Ad

STRIKE FORCE FALKLANDS
6

'WARE MINES!

Futura

A Futura Book

First published in Great Britain in 1985 by
Futura Publications, a Division of
Macdonald & Co (Publishers) Ltd, London & Sydney

ISBN 0 7088 2841 8

Photoset in North Wales by
Derek Doyle & Associates, Mold, Clwyd
Printed in Great Britain by
Hunt Barnard, Aylesbury

Futura Publications
A Division of
Macdonald & Co (Publishers) Ltd
Maxwell House
74 Worship Street
London EC2A 2EN

A BPCC plc Company

CHAPTER ONE

It was odd. In fact, it was decidedly odd, Lieutenant Miles Barker reckoned as he let rip with a rattling long burst of jimpy fire.

Special Strike Force were as rough, tough and hairy a bunch of professional fighting men as one would find in a hot spot anywhere, specially trained in covert operations in which stealth, guile, silence and invisibility ruled paramount. And here they were loosing off a storm of gunfire, creating uproar, blowing up valuable stocks of pyrotechnics, and happily destroying considerable portions of the Falklands countryside.

The Argies certainly ought to know Special Strike Force was here now.

In the last few minutes before sunrise the beach away to the left of Strike Force and the slopes ahead seemed quiet, poised as if awaiting a sign. Return fire came whickering in, entering the peaty ground with a wet sucking thud, or zinging off the rocks.

The oddness of this operation did not, of course, reside in the loudness of the bangs, or in the fact that Strike Force was making this kind of row. Blowing things up was part of its trade and they were very good at it. No. It lay in the fact that they'd more or less sat up and hollered across at the Argies: 'We're here! Yoo hoo! We're the Brits and we're here to kick your arses off the Falklands!'

'I devoutly trust,' Sergeant 'Deadly Dennis' Underhill remarked, 'that the Good Lord has seen that they're well supplied with toilet paper over there.'

'From what we've seen over on West Falklands,' replied Corporal Roger Rawson, 'the Argies do all right for supplies.'

Strike Force's own experiences confirmed this. Naturally, when the going got tougher the situation might change.

This time their own equipment actually included a mortar. Corporal Dan Taylor and Lance Corporal Ralph Hughes pumped the bombs out as fast as they could slide them into the tube. There was some degree of accuracy in the aim, but they weren't too particular. Just get the bloody things falling somewhere near the Argies, that was the idea.

Contrary to popular opinion, Special Strike Force was not keen to kill people unnecessarily.

The horizon began to flush with colour, uncertainly, like a girl who isn't quite sure if she's being insulted or not. Soon the wind, which had lain dormant during the night, would be up and would blow all day, getting down their necks and making them even colder than normal. Then the mist would blow away, but by that time Strike Force would have gone.

They didn't have any Pucaras or helicopters to whistle up, but they travelled on foot. They were more likely to be offered the chance of a ride in a Gemini than in a helicopter. So they used their natural habitat, hiding in holes where they could. They faded into the background, a technique which made their present antics all the more odd.

Incoming fire, inaccurate though it might be, was becoming unpleasant. Sooner or later an Argie bastard would poop off a clip and catch a bloke from Strike Force. Those were the odds. Miles Barker, commonly known as Barky, decided it was time for the next phase.

During the darkness they'd been moving fire positions to confuse the hostiles. They had, by their standards, been lavishly equipped with machine guns. General purpose machine guns, jimpys, were perfectly adequate for this kind of work. The linked belts of ammunition were a pain in the neck, but they did enable a nice sustained rate of fire to be maintained.

Barky had eleven men with him. He ran Number Three Wing of SSF, and they'd taken a bit of a hammering since they'd set foot on the Falklands. They had the mortar, and five machine guns. Their work load, therefore, was considerable. What the Argies thought of the current attack only concerned Barky in so far as it would encourage them to stay where they were and with any luck to call for reinforcements.

He stopped firing and hauled out his pocket Scimitar wireless set which defied interception. At his side Deadly raked another ammo case around ready to link belts.

'Dingle, SS,' called Barky. 'Now.'

Further around the arc of fire the two Smiths, Sidney and Alf, both Lance Corporals, ceased fired. Leaving the jimpy set up and ready to go, they wriggled back among the boulders. They were going to enjoy this.

The neatly-dumped explosives looked quite innocent sitting there. SS and Dingle set to work laying the charges.

In their dispersed pattern material clothing, they were not as well camouflaged in these conditions as they should have been. The indistinct flush along the skyline would not give enough light to a hostile observer to pick them out, but the Argies had high-quality American night sights. Through one of those the Brits would stand out plainly, lit by a weird green glow, and the sights would come on, the trigger finger tighten – and bam ... Highly unpleasant.

The fresh tangy smell of the sea, the nip in the air, the scent of peat and the stink of cordite complemented the work in hand. Though there might be only twelve of them acting as though they were at least a company strong, SS and Dingle were going to give the Argies more than enough to think about. The enemy might even reckon a whole flaming battalion had landed. That would be nice.

Most of the charges had been wired up as soon as they'd landed. Now it was time to make last adjustments and await Barky's signal.

The light slowly improved, a creeping wash of pearl irradiating the lowering sky. Barky flicked on his Scimitar. He was, like them all, an extremely hard and tough specimen of humanity. They were all distinct individuals in Strike Force, all men with their own quirks and idiosyncracies, their own funny little ways. Yet every one of them shared an inner toughness, a conviction that they belonged to the world's very best fighting team.

Barky was not completely bald, a few hairs clinging coyly to his scalp. Now he wore a cap for if the weather, which so far had been unusually kind, broke then he'd make damn sure his bald skull didn't lose all his body heat.

Dingle's voice rode in.

'Barky? Dingle. All set.'

'Right. Go.'

They used these nicknames not just because they were used to them and because the comradeship they engendered was real and vital. They were also a valuable form of security. Hostile ears listening in, if that were possible with the Scimitar wireless sets, would have a hard time convincing anyone that the voices they heard were genuinely a part of Strike Force.

He called out to the rest of the Wing. There was need only to give the order to go – The final series of bangs went off as the timers fired, smoke jetted into the chill dawn air, and, as though hearing a starting pistol, the men of Number Three Wing, Special Strike Force, seemed to vanish from the face of the earth.

What the Argie commander might make of their abrupt and startling disappearance, Barky couldn't know. He moved on, flat, well down, keeping in good lines of cover, aiming for the rally point.

In his usual oddball way, Deadly Dennis thought that no doubt those fascist dictators who'd set up as a junta would welcome the disappearance of the whole of the British forces. Well, those fat specimens of leeches had another think coming. At least, that was his view.

Everybody in Strike Force owned an opinion. More often than not they kept those views in a low key, preferring to get on with the job in hand; occasionally a burst of highly-coloured opinion would flare up into argument.

Less-burdened than when they landed they pulled back along the ragged crest of the beach past the Argentinian positions. Any sensible sentry expecting an invasion from the sea would look that way. He would not have been disappointed when Strike Force showed up making all manner of noise and flames. Now the invasion had petered out that sensible sentry, besides congratulating himself on winning the fight and beating off the attack, might think it would be useful to shoot a few of the British as they scuttled back to sea. So Strike Force hacked along the beach ridge, well under cover, invisible, and moving fast.

Within the strong fraternity in Strike Force – a sense of discipline and cohesion appropriate to an order of military monks, as the Major liked to point out – friendships existed of both fragility and steel. If you were too pally with a bloke and he was killed, that made a bad scene for you. But, if you didn't much care for the blokes in whom you trusted your life ...?

Deadly Dennis scuttled along the ground as though half of him was actually below the surface, and he looked anxiously at Barky. If Barky was entering one of his moods of depression right now, Deadly would have to do some jollying up.

In a brief moment in a hollow as they checked ahead and astern, Deadly began to make a veiled comment but Barky cut in, crudely, 'I don't reckon we did enough, Deadly. I'm not convinced. If I'm not convinced, how can the Argies be?'

'We pinned 'em down here, where they were supposed to be, didn't we?'

'Yeah. Reckon.'

'Well, then?'

'Just that I fancied doing a bit more on D-Day.'

'The Good Lord will –'

'Sure. And right now the maroon machine and the marines are going ashore – what's happening to them up at San Carlos? Hey?'

'Number One Wing's –' Barky scowled so fiercely that Deadly decided to shut up.

Number One Wing of Strike Force, supported by Number Two, had gone ashore with the invasion. The Major had been wounded earlier on, so the force was being led by Captain Tom Burnaby. Number Three Wing, under Barky's loving care and protection, had caught the mission to hold this gaggle of Argies where they were. The whole area had been thoroughly scouted. If stray bunches of hostiles started turning up where they were not wanted, then the planning staff would consider someone had dropped a most resounding clanger.

If some little Argie conscript with his anorak and chamber-pot of a helmet shot a British Para or Marine as they came ashore ... Kipling wrote about the disparity between the cost of educating a soldier and the cost of killing him.

Barky scratched his nose, carefully, and prepared to move on. The cost in modern warfare of killing one man ran into the millions, of course; but this little shindig in the South Atlantic bore a remarkable resemblance to the old Martini-Henry wars. Yet the differences were even more remarkable.

Roller moved out ahead; even if an Argie happened to be inspecting the terrain there the chances of his being spotted remained remote. There was always a chance, of course, and that was how blokes got killed.

The chances had run out for Stumer. He'd been killed, and no one in Strike Force would forget him. They would just soldier on.

Shrimp had come in from HQ, relieved by Noggy who was mending well after falling off a submarine. Roller and Shrimp tended to pair off as oppos within the patrol. Despite his name, Shrimp was not on the small side. Now he dogged along just to the flank and rear of Roller, hungry at the chance of at last doing something instead of being stuck on that blasted set at HQ. He knew someone had to do that job, but Shrimp was now looking forward to some real action.

Occasionally over the noise of the wind, the distant deep-throated rumble of gunfire could be distinguished. Barky was aware that other Special Forces were out convincing the Argies they were being attacked from many different directions. It sounded as though the Navy was carrying out a shoot in support.

As the day wore on the sunshine remained bright and piercing; damned unusual weather, considered Barky. His job was half done. They'd convinced the hostiles that the attack was in sufficient strength for them to stay where they were and the Argies had not pulled back to rush up to San Carlos.

It remained to prevent the Argies actually going to San Carlos, if they decided on that course of action.

Without really thinking about it, everyone in the Wing was looking for a good ambush site. At this distance from the landing point they could hack along a little more freely. They were fearsomely burdened down, for although a sizeable proportion of the ammo had been shot off sufficient remained for a battle. Under huge loads, their jaguar packs bulging, they drove on.

Up ahead around San Carlos the other Special Forces, which had been ashore for some time, would be welcoming the troops landing ashore. Just what Number One Wing of Strike Force was actually doing at this time Barky didn't know. He knew he'd have to decide on a good spot soon though. If the Argies they'd shot along the beach were ordered to resist the landing then they'd be along quite soon.

By then Strike Force would be dug in, invisible, their weaponry ready to contest any hostile movement.

Major Dan Granville, who'd created Strike Force and had inculcated the lads with his own methods, had done that work well. As Barky carefully crested a slight ridge and saw the lie of the land, he knew this was the place. The others, in their turn, also recognised its salient features, the channeling effect of the land, the potential killing zones, the neat avenue of escape.

Barky humped off his jaguar pack. 'Right,' he said, and that was enough.

One of the Major's pet sayings which circulated among the members of SSF was simply: 'Your job is to ambush the enemy; not get ambushed yourself.' The maxim was devoutly believed in by everyone in Strike Force.

In performing this very necessary function, Barky, for one and not alone, found the fascination lay in using his skill in selecting the site and laying out the positions. Interlocking zones of fire were obvious, of course; but the subtler cunning of channeling hostiles where you wanted them to go presented the real challenge. Strike Force might normally be an observation unit; when events became hot then they'd be a hit and run mob. This cold-blooded preparation for a holding action brought a tingle to the tips of the ears, a quiver of new interest.

The big wireless set was dumped down with the mortar team to the rear of the position.

Sweeping the field of view of his glasses over the opposite slope, cutting along the ridge down to the dip and then up again, Barky made a mark of assent himself. The machine guns were sited. The mortar could drop a few nasties where they'd do the most good. He had no mines or barbed wire so the Argies would be spared those.

One thing he was very sure of. He would not hang around here for a moment longer than necessary. Once the Task Force had put the troops ashore and they had set themselves up in the bridgehead, then they would be perfectly capable of taking care of themselves. If this bunch of Argies ran into the Paras, say, or the Marines – well, they'd regret it. That was for sure.

A flicker of movement over on the ridge crest. A dark blob, moving ... Barky settled himself.

'Right,' he said to himself. 'Right, my old son. Here they come.'

CHAPTER TWO

Over on West Falkland WOII Arthur Fuller and Sergeant Jack Dexter crept along like a couple of Red Indians on the warpath.

Dexter remained firmly convinced that Punch Fuller should not have been allowed to have his own way. The big fellow had simply insisted on going on the operation and there had been no way of talking him out of it. Punch had been struck over the head by an Argentine rifle butt, and Dexter was not at all convinced that he had recovered from the blow.

When they'd rejoined the unit after the most recent fracas they'd learned the shattering news that Major Dan Granville had been wounded, was out of the action and had been hospitalised back to the S.S. *Uganda*. The news depressed everyone in Strike Force; everything conspired to make the lads think of the Major and remember his funny ways.

Punch and Dexter were secreted in a hollow under the camouflage of their ponchos, and they kept up an obbo on the bunch of Argentinians below. Everything the two comrades did reminded them of the Major.

The brightness of the sunshine, however unseasonal, couldn't disguise its hollow chill or mitigate the effects of the howling Falklands wind. The Argies were up to something – as they so often were since their forceful theft of the islands – and Dexter and Punch wanted to know just what that was.

The Major, for all his funny ways, insisted on absolute accuracy in a report. Without the facts, he'd say, you can't net 'em and drag 'em.

'They intend to stay there.' Punch took the glasses from his eyes. 'Lotta kit.'

'Yeah.'

'Stop worrying, Joker! I'm perfectly all right.'

'Sure.'

'Look, you can probe my skull if you like. See?' Here Punch shoved his woolly cap up and bent his head.

Dexter, generally known as the Joker, sat back in the hole. 'Knock it off, Punch!'

The real trouble was that in a bunch of fighting men you couldn't afford to make a true-blue friend, a comrade for whom you felt the pangs you felt for yourself. The Major's system insisted that everyone in Strike Force was an oppo to everyone else. That meant that any of them could work as a team together. Dexter and Punch usually formed a team, and Dexter knew he felt far more for Punch than he'd allow lightly even to his own consciousness.

If you disliked or hated the men with whom you worked and fought, said one theory, then the adrenalin flowed and the unit functioned on antipathy. The Major felt that to be a less effective system than his own.

Some of the blokes in Strike Force could get right up Dexter's nose. But he trusted every one of them implicitly. Even Rommel.

'Gonna be a long job.' Since the blow on his head

Punch, usually the most taciturn of men, tended to chatter.

'Yeah,' said Dexter.

Punch shoved his cap back. His face, like Dexter's might have stood in for a granite obelisk, and his toughness have scared a giant; he was a fellow into the business of helping little old ladies across the road. He had his priorities in life worked out. At the moment, under orders, he and Dexter kept up an obbo on stupid thieving Argies and tried to suss out exactly what they were up to.

Some fellows with alert and active minds might find keeping observation boring. The blokes in Strike Force did not see it in that light. There was always something to be learned. If they fouled up on what appeared to be a simple obbo job, they could end up being killed. That risk tended to sober the mind.

At least Dexter could take some form of comfort from Punch's failure to wangle himself into the main body of Number Three Wing. They were across on East Falkland creating merry hell and scaring the Argies into thinking they were the invasion. Or that was the theory ...

Punch's obstinacy had got himself here, bash on the head or no bash on the head. So Dexter had come along as well. He and Punch were a team. Goddamnit.

'What the hell are they doin', Joker?'

'Dunno.'

'I think I'll stir 'em up a trifle. Get the old bowels working.'

'You do that, Punch, and you'll –'

'Yeah. I know. Still and all.'

Jack the Joker Dexter refused to be drawn.

For a time they waited and watched in silence. The

wind keened across the empty land. There wasn't a single damned tree in the whole of the Falklands. That seemed to Dexter right against Nature. That was right out of order, that was.

The smell of wetness and dampness, even in this bright sunshine, seeped in from everywhere; the peaty ground, the bluster of the wind, and the barely-heard susurration of the sea over the rise. A bloke could go mouldy in this climate. Even though Dexter and Punch wore privately-purchased mountain-cum-hiking boots, they knew that spending too long like this would cause their boots to rot and fall off. Other things would rot and fall off if a bloke spent too much time down here in the South Atlantic ...

Just as Dexter started to let his mind dwell lasciviously on Patsy and the way she apparently didn't mind letting the whole world gawp at the magnificence of her body, Punch began to jabber again.

'Lotta barrels down there, Joker. Reckon they're putting a fuel dump together.'

'Could be.'

'D'you reckon they're trying tanks?'

'On this terrain? You off your chump?'

As soon as he had spoken Dexter wished he hadn't. Punch would take the remark in the way it was meant. That was all right. But it brought uncomfortably close to the surface the real fears Dexter entertained about his oppo. That crack on the head *could* have seriously scrambled Punch's brains, have shorted out vital synapses, have blown more than one fuse.

Punch snorted a very un-Punchlike laugh.

'They'd need submersible tanks here, right enough.'

'Yeah.'

Punch remained frisky. He did not fidget. A member of Strike Force on an obbo knew how to keep still. But he was on edge in what he said, in the fretful way he spoke, the way he kept on twitching his arm as though to lift himself up and put a burst of fire into the Argies below.

About to open a line of small talk, to which Punch was increasingly becoming addicted, Dexter opened his mouth and then snapped it shut as Punch belted out, 'Aircraft!'

The two men froze.

Then Punch added out of the corner of his mouth, 'Keep tha' haid dahn, laddie.'

Dexter felt a chill of apprehension for his comrade, and then the two aircraft whistled past, dragging his thoughts into their proper channel.

'Two Argie bleeding Skyhawks,' said Punch.

Dexter's impression had been of two fleeting images, vague and indistinct, flashing past. A hint of camouflage painting rather than overall grey or blue, a wedge-shaped wing they had not seen in plain view, a solid looking tail. A couple of Argie A4s, Skyhawks, on the prowl and boding no Brit any good.

Then Punch sucked in a breath. Dexter saw it, too. They stared at each other. They spoke together.

'*Harriers*!'

Neither man felt any doubt.

The air intakes on a Harrier ought to make identification instant and absolute; yet the A4's air intakes, although smaller and mounted higher, could be mistaken when the aeroplane was hurtling along like a bat out of hell. Dexter's lips curled a trifle. He fancied the pilots in all the air forces down here thought of themselves as winging along like bats out of hell. It was a natural conceit.

'RAF, not Navy,' said Punch.

'Yeah.'

'Ground attack.'

'They must have missed it, then.'

At one time Dexter had been a voracious reader of science fiction, absorbing it in huge quantities and quite uncaring of quality. He'd been particularly attracted by space opera, relishing the grandeur and scope, even the grandiose aspects of the form. Then all those silly sci-fi films had come along and ruined it all. The point was that now he felt personally affronted that he could not flick a switch on his radio and call up the pilots of the Harriers. Then he could have called them in to have a crack at the fuel dump the Argies were stockpiling.

By the time he called Noggy at HQ on the big set and he organised his liaison with the RAF, the two Harriers would be long gone, well on their way back to their Royal Navy hosts aboard the carriers.

He swivelled his eyes to take in the part of sky where the Harriers had vanished. There was little chance the Argies would spot the two Brits in their hide; but a bloke in Strike Force did not take stupid chances. Movement was kept to a minimum.

The sky remained its unseasonally brilliant blue. The breeze blew as usual. There was no sign of the Harriers returning.

'Those Brylcreem Boys,' Punch was saying, savouring the old words, untrue though they might be. 'They couldn't –'

His words were drowned by a crescendo shrieking in the air, and then the sense of hurtling bodies, the sudden rush and shadow of wings and four huge explosions.

Dexter just had a glimpse of the pair of Harriers

screaming past before the edge of the fuel dump was blotted out in black and red and orange. Black oily smoke pulsed in billows into the sky. Barrels, burning, smoking, flew everywhere. The noise clamoured on and on.

Dexter recalled Captain Tom Burnaby remarking back in England that the Harrier was a friendly aircraft, rather like an elephant, a jumbo plane with big flapping air intakes. This pair were Harriers GR.3, the RAF version. They had that odd scooped-looking nose cone, unlike the sharper cone of the Sea Harriers. They seemed to Dexter to have lost any sense of being cheerful, jumbo-like planes. Now they were hard, lethal, purposeful. Their dark green and mid-grey camouflage blended in well as they flew past. With a typical screeching whistling roar they hurtled over and were gone.

After a bit, as the fires below burned luridly into the brightness of the day, Punch said, 'One up for the Brylcreem Boys, Joker.'

'Yeah.'

'Save us a job.'

'P'raps.'

'Well, no good hanging about here, is it?'

'Maybe there's –'

'One thing, though, Joker. They did us out of blowing up the dump. Stopped us from making our own nice big bang.'

'I was going to say maybe they didn't get it all. Some oil drums might be left for you to have fun with.'

'After that little lot?'

'Maybe.'

Punch knew his oppo the Joker Dexter of old.

'Hang around, then, and see?'

'Yeah.'

Down below across the boggy slope the Argentinians were going crazy. They were rushing about like blue bottle flies, as Punch said.

'Turdheads,' he said, forcefully. 'Serves 'em right.'

The dump blazed and crackled and belched black smoke. Dexter began to doubt that anything could be left unburned.

Punch's face, as hard a lump of granite as Dexter's own, glared down on the scene of destruction. Presently he said: 'Reckon he ought to mosey along and then come back the other way. Get closer down to the beach. Might be some pickings.'

Their duty to observe and report on the Argentinians did not preclude them from blowing up the Argies if the chance came along. Dexter was only too well aware that Punch wouldn't be satisfied until he had, personally, had a hand in spectacular destruction.

'Check.'

Packing up a hide in daylight could be a tricky job. Now both men felt every confidence that the hostiles were too busy trying to put out the fires to spare a glance up into the rocks and ridges across the swampy slope.

The two ponchos came down and were rolled neatly and stowed, the kit was hoisted and settled about their persons, and with weapons in fists they sloped off in the opposite direction. Just how far Punch would be patient enough to go before he cut towards the sea and started the return trip Dexter didn't know.

He did know Punch Fuller would cut the time down as much as possible. Burning on a short fuse right now was Punch Fuller.

Punch prowled on ahead with Dexter slightly to the

rear and flank. He sped along like a man with a mission. Popular imagery, Dexter often felt, would liken him to a great hunting cat silently stalking his prey in the jungle. Well, there was truth in that.

The sea looked unpleasant, slatey and heaving queasily; but every now and again a slanting shaft of light caught the top of a wave and sent a brilliant sparkle up into the air to dazzle the eyes. This unexpected good weather couldn't last much longer. Snow was around somewhere.

Coils of black smoke continued to rise along the beach. Dexter felt an odd little twinge of amusement as Punch halted, looked back, and said, 'About now, Joker.'

'Yeah.'

'Can't let the Brylcreem Boys have all the fun.'

'Fun,' said Dexter. 'Come on, Punch.'

Both men knew exactly what Dexter was on about.

'Well, hell,' rumbled Punch. 'Y'know –'

'Sure. Only I'm the Joker Dexter. I'm not some little tabloid newspaper.'

All Punch could say was: 'Check.'

Moving with the consummate skill of masters of their art, they wormed forward into the new obbo position. From here, among tumbled boulders along the fringe of the beach, they had a fair view of the dump and the fire.

Further along the curve of the beach ended in a headland. Here the cliffs fell sheer to the sea. Normally the place would be alive with the flutter and turmoil of sea birds. Now, with a war going on, many of the birds had sensibly taken themselves off to healthier parts.

'Sod all doing here, Joker.'

The dump, blazing and boiling black smoke, obscured direct vision along the beach. It looked as though it might burn for hours yet.

'Yeah,' said Dexter. He swivelled his glasses along the curve of the beach, around the rear of the smoke cloud. He could see no sign of life anywhere.

Tilting the glasses he looked around and up. The coarse grasses and clumps of rock slid past in a dun blur. He focused on the crest of the cliffs.

'Check the cliff top, Punch.'

Together, they concentrated on the little black figures up there.

'What the hell are they up to *now*?' demanded Punch, exasperated at these carryings-on and itching to blow something up.

Before Dexter could frame a politic answer, a helicopter whirred up into sight like a partridge breaking cover. It hovered over the cliff top and then alighted, the vanes glinting. The sound of the chopper's engine and blades barely reached them through the slosh and rush of the sea.

'Sea King,' said Punch.

'Yeah. Argie version.'

She was a Sikorsky the Argentinians called an S-61D-4, operated by the Aviacion Naval Argentina. She settled down, the vanes whirred to a stillness, and the small back figures of men closed about her.

'The turdheads are up to something, that's for sure.'

'Can't see nothing from here.'

'Nah. Have to take a recce over there.'

Dexter checked the sun and then his watch.

'We can hack it just before nightfall, I reckon,' he said.

'Easy.' Punch sounded much more cheerful. 'We have an objective, my son. We are going to pay those little snot noses a visit, and if they've left their chopper out for us to play with – luvverly!'

CHAPTER THREE

The hack around inland had to be conducted with skill and care. Punch and Dexter, their tiger-striped faces intent, moved along at a good pace. They conserved their energy for what might lie ahead. The ground proved its usual boggy self and they had to accept some bad going to avoid crests and skylines.

And, all the time they scanned the sky for the first sign of a chopper or a Pucara, their ears alert for the first betraying engine notes.

Like the rest of his comrades in Strike Force under the magic of the Major's tuition, Dexter found he could, as it were, split his brain into two parts.

At the same time as he assiduously scanned the sky and the horizon line and listened out for the first sound of hostiles, he could in a small and private part of his mind dwell on happier times.

Dexter knew that to a man like Punch there were probably no happier times than these. Punch relished the challenge of the stalk, finding the quarry, and then blowing it sky high.

But oh, no. He was not day dreaming. Proof of that came very easily.

Dexter had a clear picture of Patsy with her negligée

swirling about her, laughing and calling him to the balcony of their hotel. The fierce Spanish sun shone about them. The sea sparkled blue and silver and sailboats flitted about, wind-surfers frolicked, and rows of half-naked bodies lay along the beach broiling away amid myriad sun umbrellas. He smelled the intoxicating scent of Patsy as he strolled over to stand at her shoulder.

He put his arm about her waist and his hand felt the excitingly rounded swell of her stomach, not too much, but not as flat as a board, just right for a real woman.

'Not that, Jack, not right now – look!'

One of the little sailboats had overturned and a motor boat was wallowing about making ineffectual attempts to pull the people out of the water.

'Bunch of wallies,' said Dexter, sniffing.

He shifted his hand and Patsy laughed and leaned back into him and the clittering clattering chop-chip-chop sent him full length into the nearest scrappy bush.

Punch glared up from an adjacent clump of the coarse orange-green vegetation.

'Blasted thing's running away! Musta known we were coming for 'em.'

'Hope not,' grunted Dexter, still as a flatfish in his bush.

'Yeah.'

The Sea King lifted away, roaring, and vanished to the west.

Dexter crawled out.

'If,' said Punch in his pugnacious way, joining his oppo, 'you'd brought a blowpipe along, Joker, we could've –'

'You can carry the thing, Punch, if ever we do.'

'Oh, sure.'

They lay back a little, getting their breath back.

With Punch's alarming new habit of jabbering away at the slightest opportunity, Dexter wasn't really surprised at what his oppo came out with next.

'Was just thinking of Sharon. Y'know, Joker, we had a good time out there in Spain.'

'After,' pointed out Dexter, 'you settled up the business of the fish and chips.'

'Yeah.' There was no need for either of them to elaborate. That was closed up. 'Still, I think I could find something to do if Sharon was around now.'

'Big girl.'

'Yeah, you had to duck sharpish.'

'Plenty of practice around here, now.'

'Only difference is, then you didn't mind if you got hit.'

'Wrap it up, Punch.'

'And you.'

So, beginning a nice comfortable wrangle, they started off again, their senses alert and their nerve-endings painfully naked to every message on the air.

'Mind you,' said Dexter, prepared to mollify his comrade just a trifle, 'Mind you, that was a sight better than old Colonel Gunjepoo.'

'Thought he called himself a general.'

'Yeah. General, colonel, nobody seemed to know what to call the old buzzard.'

The fuel dump continued to burn. Black smoke lay athwart the air like thunderclouds. The two men of Strike Force pushed on, giving the Argies a wide berth in which to play at being firemen.

Every now and then they halted to take a recce of their surroundings, notably of the inland side of the headland ahead. Featureless in many respects the Falklands may be; the rock formations around here were interesting not only to a geologist but to a man who needed to find a hole in a hurry.

From White Rock Bay in the north southwards to Fox Bay was about forty five miles and a helicopter could cover that distance in around twenty minutes. The two Strike Force oppos moved out with extreme caution, ready to jump for a welcoming hole or friendly bush at every step.

Dexter's prediction as to time proved correct and they found themselves a nice little hole as the last of the light fell across the desolate land. Very quickly they converted the new place into a tidy little hide, brewed up, stuffed rations down inside, and then started to sort out what was going and what they could leave in the hide.

'Better give Noggy a call and tell him what's going down,' said Punch.

Dexter didn't bother to reply but got the big scimitar going and called HQ.

'All right, Joker,' said Noggy after Dexter had explained. 'Keep me informed. And keep your heads down.' Then he added mysteriously, 'Fireworks are due.'

'Check.'

Punch had no doubt what Noggy meant. 'The show's on,' he said in his confident way. There was no chance of mistaking what Noggy had said. If they'd been forced into keying Morse there might have been room for doubt; Punch rubbed his hands together.

'The Task Force has at last made up its collective little minds.' Punch's ferocious face twisted bitterly, as he added, 'They ain't going ashore at Stanley, I can tell you that. Let's hope Stumer fooled the buggers.'

'If he did, his death helped.'

About to go on and burst out that he wondered if the death of a comrade could be warranted by the repossession of a few bits of land stuck out in the middle of nowhere in the South Atlantic, Dexter held his tongue. The time for recriminations and post mortems would come later. Right now their task was to help regain the Falklands from the pack of thieving bastards who'd stolen them. One day, no doubt, in some more perfect future, the Brits and the no-longer thieving bastards could get together to talk the situation over. That time was not now in the middle of a shooting war.

His reflective mood brought to mind the question of shooting Argies. Dexter for one, and others in Strike Force, saw, if not clearly then with an attempt at grasping the problem, that indiscriminate killing would not be beneficial in the long term. Oh yes, of course they might have to mallet a few of the hostiles along the way; but their instructions remained specific on achieving their aims with the minimum of death and destruction.

If some poor little sod of an Argie could be knocked over and tied up or put out of action without killing him, then that was their aim now. The death of one poor little scared Argie would not sway the greater design – unless that man happened to stand, as it were, foursquare across the objectives of Strike Force.

Mind you, Dexter was well aware that these views did not necessarily reflect those of the whole of Special Strike Force. Punch now – if an Argie got in his way then self-preservation, the lives of his comrades and the achievement of the object must come first.

The star-studded night was clear and frosty. They saddled up and moved out when it was fully dark.

Objects took on their usual ghostly form, indistinct masses against the gloom. The lack of trees in the Falklands meant they didn't have to worry about distinguishing between a sentry watching them or the stump of a tree. They moved out with caution. When communication was necessary they used hand signals or barely audible whispers that carried from mouth to ear and no further.

The ground became firmer as they approached the inward curve of the headland. They made no noise. On a night like this sound could travel for miles. The breeze had died away.

Up ahead and to the flank, Punch halted.

Instantly, Dexter dropped to a knee. His rifle snouted, the Enfield Individual Weapon beautifully balanced, snug, ready to let rip. He breathed quietly and evenly, hardly aware of the rasp of the cold air.

After a few moments, Punch moved on out. Dexter followed. He watched the dim figure ahead and only occasionally checked further beyond, most of his attention taken by the flanks and rear and by keeping tabs on Punch.

Again Punch halted. Dexter stopped.

Punch's hand flicked in a brief gesture. Obediently, Dexter, doubled over, scurried up to drop down beside his oppo.

'Keep seeing shadows up ahead.'

Dexter waited. If Punch said he saw shadows, then Punch saw shadows. They were probably the dim outlines of hostiles. They hunkered down for ten minutes.

Then Punch said: 'There.'

The starlight spread a rind of silver on the round

shape ahead of them further up the slope.

'Bleeding Argie helmet.'

'Yeah.'

'We'll have to take him.'

Punch didn't wait. He was up and moving forward crouched over, Sterling snouting, covering ground at a ferocious rate. He angled off slightly to his left. The inevitable sound of boots on the ground could only be reduced by as much as his skill, training and experience could contrive. The Argie heard him at the very last minute. In that moment Punch launched himself headlong.

His knobbly left fist swept in a vicious arc. He cannoned into the hostile. They both collapsed, the Argie underneath, Punch on top and already rolling away.

The Argentinian soldier lay sprawled and still. Punch's eyeballs swivelled, left, right and centre.

Now the sound of the sea broke in rolling splashings upon the silence. If the enemy up there had that in their ears all the time they could easily hear through it. Punch waited.

The Argie had occupied a small scrape and in one corner a litter of cigarette butts told their own story. He'd been sitting down to have a spit and a draw, and had stood up to peek over the top every now and again. Punch looked around. He could see no sign of barbed wire. He just hoped there were no mines.

At Punch's signal Dexter joined him.

'There's gotta be more'n this one bloke.'

'Yeah.'

Punch sounded dubious, most unlike him.

'Bash straight on, or check laterals?'

'They've not spotted us.'

'Far as we know.'

'Oh – sure.'

'The quicker we get in,' said Dexter, 'the quicker we get out. In theory.'

Punch's reaction to the fatuous remark was typical. He jerked a thumb at the unconscious Argentinian. 'This bloke –'

'This,' broke in Dexter, 'ain't World War Two and he ain't a Nazi. Tie him up.'

'Gag him, too. But good.'

'Check.'

The men of Strike Force carried lengths of cord for just this purpose. Barky, everyone knew, always carried an inordinately long piece, and he'd been kidded about this from time to time.

'Ah, my lads,' he'd say with a twinkle. 'One day you'll see.'

Now Dexter expertly lashed up the Argie and made him as comfortable as possible. By the time the Brits had finished their recce the man's comrades would have discovered and freed him.

Keeping very low, squirming along, they moved out. Then, in the blessed way half-trained troops have of advertising their presence to opposing ears and noses, the sound of voices up ahead reached the Brits, together with the unmistakable smell on the frosty air of some exotic South American foodstuff. Dexter sniffed.

'Doing 'emselves proud.'

'All bleeding garlic rubbish, I expect.'

'All right in its place.'

Creeping along over the ground they circled the source of the advertising.

'Four of 'em?'

'Yeah.'

In the next instant Punch halted. Dexter hauled up and then inched forward alongside his oppo. Both men could see strands of barbed wire barring their forward progress.

'Blast it. Wire!'

'Tin cans with stones, too.'

'Yeah.'

The wire was not in thick coils but neatly arranged on stakes, the topmost strands about chest high.

Dexter was carrying the cutters. There would be a slight problem cutting through so as not to disturb the alarm cans. The mischief lay in the return journey.

Punch started to say something else, and Dexter put a hand on his arm. He squeezed. This frightening habit of Punch's of jabbering all the time had to be stopped before an Argie with ears heard them and raised the alarm.

Punch's rumble sounded ominously loud.

'They can't hear us, Joker, for Pete's sake!'

Dexter did not reply, just went on snipping the strands of wire. He cut a gap and then motioned to Punch to hold a tin can whilst he cut it away from the wire holding it dangling, ready to rattle its damnfool head off.

They put the tin carefully upon the ground well away from the cut gap.

Neither man considered traversing one way or the other to attempt to reach the end of the wire. They both sensed the Argentinians had fenced off the whole end of the headland. Something was up here that was of value, and Strike Force wanted to know exactly what that might be.

Bulky yet moving like an alley cat, Punch started forward.

A smashing crescendo of bullets slapped down about him and the night resounded with the clatter of gunfire.

Without hesitation Punch was flat, nose into the ground, spread out like a flatfish. In the same motion he wriggled back and flopped down flat again.

'The turdheads! Night sight.'

'Yeah.'

Punch's reaction to this insult was to unclip a grenade. Whether or not Dexter wanted to go along with this answer, if he had an opinion on the matter, was of no consequence. Punch heaved his arm over and the grenade sailed away.

The explosion crashed out with violent loudness into the night. After the silence the harsh rattle of machine gun fire had assaulted the ears, but now the grenade demolished them. In the bellow of the concussion and the outward flare of light, Punch and Dexter squiggled away wormlike, low and sinuous and keeping their heads down.

A single piercing scream screeched after them.

The machine gun hammered again, lacing the ground at random. The volley persisted as the two members of Strike Force rolled into a little hollow. Their breathing remained even and steady, but their tempers were frayed and Punch was clearly on the verge of an explosion.

'I'd like to –' he started.

'Yeah. Wrap it up. More of 'em about.'

'Sure. Check. Just that –'

'Punch!'

'My head, Joker. Hurts.'

A thundering crash off to the right sobered Dexter.

The Argies had tossed a grenade at the British. Tit for tat, that, no doubt, was what they thought.

'We've gotta get out of here,' he said, making the words vicious, trying to jolly Punch along. The big fellow did not look good. His face had taken on an impression of length, as though the muscles and sinews drew it down lugubriously.

'My head, Joker.'

Another Argie grenade exploded away to their left.

'C'mon, Punch.'

Dexter put a hand under his comrade's armpit and hoisted him up. Punch staggered, his left hand groping uncertainly, like that of a blind man feeling for support and contact. Dexter kept a grip on him and they moved downslope together.

The third grenade, pitched between the first two, sent both men tumbling forward into cover. They waited, ears ringing.

'I'd like to –' mumbled Punch.

His left hand wrapped around Dexter's forearm. Dexter felt the grip and pressure there. He understood Punch was fighting a battle within himself. Aware of their mutual esteem, their comradeship, Dexter knew he could say nothing.

'We'll get back to the hide,' he said. He rose, cautiously as ever. One could never relax at night when Argie American-supplied night sights were in use. 'C'mon.'

'No.'

'Huh?'

'Nope. I ain't running off. I'm gonna –'

'Punch!'

'It's no good, Joker. I'm not standing for this. I'm

going to go back up there and blow those turdheads away.'

'That's not on. Not now.'

'It sure as hell is!'

Punch Fuller had fought his own private battle. Being Punch Fuller he'd reached the only conclusion he could and remain in character. He might have been struck viciously on the head by a rifle butt, and he might have been concussed, have temporarily gone blind. His head might hurt. But he was Punch Fuller. He wasn't going to be scared off just because a bunch of miserable turdhead Argies bunged a few grenades at him, was he?

'Punch!'

'You coming, then, Joker? Or not? Never needed to ask before.'

'I'll come if we go –'

'Straight into 'em before they know what's hit 'em.'

'There's a night sight up there, a machine gun and grenade-happy hostiles.'

'Then I'll be off on my own, Joker, and I'm sorry ...'

Punch's voice thickened. His voice trailed away, husking into a throaty silence. He put an unsteady hand to his head.

'Joker, my bloody head's on fire! It's falling off.'

Dexter did the the only thing he could. He put his fist cleanly and with precision against Punch's jaw and he caught the big fellow as he fell down.

That settled the argument. Only for the moment, though, only for the moment ...

CHAPTER FOUR

'Here they come!'

Barky lined up the sights of the machine gun. The wind blew about his ears and the cap over his almost-bald head comforted him.

Now if he'd had a few Claymores to spread along the route the Argies were taking he could have triggered the devastating mines and delivered nasty chunks of metal in wide areas – that would have made the hostiles stop and think.

They came on down the slope, spread out but not spread out enough to please a soldier trained up by Major Dan Granville. There would be no need to give any orders. Strike Force would attack as one unit.

'Reckon they're just moseying along following us,' said Deadly Dennis. 'They don't expect to find us.'

'If,' Barky said, oddly thankful for the relief of saying something, 'you come out with something like "and the Lord has delivered them into our hand," I'll, I'll, I dunno what I'll do.'

'Shoot 'em, that's what.'

Barky's lips compressed. He didn't want to kill anyone, including these poor Argies. Of course he would if he had to, to save his own or a comrade's life. But he wouldn't just cut the hostiles down. He wouldn't blast them away as they trotted along in the open.

He realised he could be making a mistake. But he pressed the trigger in the belief that, mistaken or not, he was doing the right thing.

The rounds rattled through the jimpy. Strikes gouged into the soggy ground. The other jimpys opened up and the Argies simply pell-melled, struggling to get out of one another's way, dropping flat, running away like maniacs back up the slope, or trying to squirm off to one side. It was quite a sight.

Barky stopped firing. The other machine guns fell silent. No mortar bombs had been shot off. Silence dropped down.

'As an ambush,' said Deadly, suffering, 'I've seen better.' He glanced accusingly at Barky.

'We stopped 'em.'

'Maybe. But you aimed to miss.'

'Sure.'

Barky was perfectly confident and unrepentent.

'If they –'

'Then we do.'

'Check!'

Deadly's tone of voice left no possibility of misunderstanding either his feeling or his intentions in this matter. Because he wanted to shift the point of discussion, Barky said: 'How many d'you make 'em?'

'Company. Short company.'

'Check. If they set up support weapons we move at once.'

There had been no need to say that. Barky felt himself fighting the mood of depression that often overcame him in silly moments, moments when he wanted to be alert and on the top line. He studied the opposite slope. The Argies were setting about gathering their wits and reorganising themselves.

From a clump of the widespread orange-green vegetation a tongue of fire spat out accusingly. The clattering noise of a machine gun spat in the air. Bullets thudded into the ground along the slope before Strike Force.

On the right flank SS and Dingle opened up. There was only need to put in a short burst of fire. The Argentinian machine gun came to an abrupt halt.

On the opposite slope men were cowering down, trying to scrape themselves enough cover to get their heads down. One or two took the chance of running back for the crest of the slope. The first two were chopped down by accurate fire, and then Barky called out on the scimitar to let the poor bleeders go.

Whoever the next one to run might be, he was either an hero or an idiot.

Hero or idiot, he sprinted up the slope, arms and legs pumping. His big round helmet fell off and tumbled down. He took no notice and fairly flew up to vanish over the crest.

The lads of Strike Force gave him a cheer.

'Watch the flanks,' called Barky. He was aware of what this play-acting might lead to, even in men as highly trained as those under his command.

For a time nothing more happened. Barky felt confident enough that the Argies would not make a frontal assault up the slope against five machine guns. That would be suicide. So they'd try to work around the flanks. If they had support weapons they'd be unlimbering and setting up right now. Mortars might be expected at any moment.

Decisions, decisions. Should he hold on here, or fade

away and pull back to a fresh ambush site?

Another Argie machine gun opened up and as though that were a signal the men in their scrapes began to shoot. Most of the incoming went nowhere, but Strike Force returned the fire in a careful, ammunition-husbanding way.

Barky made up his mind.

'On the flanks,' he called out over the wireless. 'Pull back a hundred. Centre hold.'

The manoeuvre was carried through with unthinking competence. The flank teams pulled back. When they reported set, Barky ordered out the three centre teams. The mortar crew went back. One moment machine gun fire was hammering away from the British crest; the next the slope lay silent as the grave.

'They'll wait a moment before coming on,' Barky was saying.

His voice was drowned by the explosion of mortar bombs. They fell haphazardly along the crest, some falling short and some overreaching.

'That's four tubes, at least!'

'Check. Saddle up. Let's get going.'

Smoke and debris pulsed up from the ridge.

The noise chased Strike Force as they hoisted their burdens and set smartly off. They did not dally.

Well, said Barky to himself as he humped along, at least it's better to fight a delaying action than a last ditch resistance stand. This way, at least, survival was a distinct possibility.

The chill Falklands' wind ruffled across the land, making conditions if not unbearable then at least unpleasant.

They'd now shot off a considerable quantity of their

ammunition. Whilst this lightened their loads, it brought up the problem of adequate firepower. Barky had no intention of allowing his command to be forced into a position of having to stand and fight. That wasn't the *modus operandi* of Strike Force. If they weren't out on an obbo job then they could hit and run, sting and fly like mosquitoes. There would be ammo enough for that.

He didn't bother to think what might have occurred if they'd not vacated the ridge before the mortar bombs sailed down. There was no point in using his imagination in that direction.

There was profit in trying to suss out what the Argentine commander was doing now.

The flanks, now. Well, yes. Barky had those monitored. Point hacked along in the centre. What was left of Number Three Wing could be called the main body, and they made their way along acting as centre and rearguard.

The distant buzzing, reminding one of a bumblebee on a hot summer's day in England, told Barky what the Argentinian commander's imagination had turned up. Pucaras.

He experienced a flash of pleasure at the Argies' bravery. If those Pucaras were bounced by Harriers, there'd be heaps of junk burning on the ground, and the wrecks would not be Harriers.

Mind you, there was no sign of a single Harrier about. Strike Force had to go invisible, and at once.

Without any fuss Strike Force seemed to disappear, submerging itself into the Falklands countryside.

The dissatisfaction nagging away at Barky ever since the landing and the deception persisted. Sure, he'd held the Argies in place, and whether or not he'd convinced them they were facing the real invasion did not matter. They'd reacted as required. Now they'd been held up. But, as far as he knew, they were still coming on. He knew damn well that he hadn't done enough.

With Deadly Dennis in a little scrape, their ponchos fixed edge to edge above them, he listened and watched as the Pucara flew over.

'Kinda nice in the sight of the Lord to let him have a few,' offered Deadly. His tiger-striped face reflected a benign desire to shoot down hostile aeroplanes.

'Yeah. But you know what Number One Wing reported.'

'I do. Napalm. An abomination and an offence in the sight of the Lord. Sod the bastards.'

'See if you can spot what he's carrying.'

They squinted up through tiny gaps between the ponchos.

The Pucara's greyish-white undersurfaces were pointed with a broad yellow Argentinian identification stripe. The tail also carried a yellow band.

Concentrating fiercely on what he could see in the fleeting time available, Barky saw the two clusters of three bombs slung under the Pucara's fuselage. The wings carried bulbous tanks, with a small fin on the outboard side.

Long range tanks or napalm?

Tanks, decided Barky, and the Pucara whistled past above, its engine note reaching a crescendo and then fading into a Doppler whine.

One thing was certain. Unless the Pucara carried sophisticated IR equipment the observer was not going to detect the presence of Strike Force below.

The engine note died.

'Give him five minutes,' said Barky. 'Then saddle up.'

'Check.'

The Pucara did not return and twenty minutes later Strike Force were well away from the area, hacking on with a determination to get ahead of the Argies and then, if they insisted on proceeding, of ambushing them again. Strongly feeling that he had not done enough, Barky knew he had to discourage the hostiles. He gave them full marks for bravery. There had to be some way of holding them in check and keeping them away from the bridgehead until the troops there were all set.

The next convenient ambush site consisted of a straggle of rocks, a boggy defile, a reasonable escape route and fields of fire that, whilst not perfect, would give enough coverage to hold a force of the size following them.

'Set up shop,' said Barky.

He arranged the set-up differently this time. Conscious of his flanks and the smallness of his own force, he had to make a pint fill a quart pot. He remained convinced that the hostiles would not advance successfully against the fire of five machine guns; but if they dropped their mortar bombs on his positions accurately and rapidly enough he could be in trouble.

If the Argies knocked out a couple of jimpy teams ... He had to think of unpleasant eventualities like that. It was a part of command.

'Wide on the flanks,' he told the teams of SS and Dingle, and of Roller and Shrimp. 'If they try to be smart and flank us either way, you enfilade 'em up their posteriors. Check?'

'Check.'

Number Three Wing of Strike Force, outwardly invisible, settled down.

This was cat and mouse stuff. If a bloke didn't get his mental machinery in order it would be highly nerve-wracking. The men of Strike Force could not allow mundane problems like nerves to interfere with their work. They were, after all, professionals.

All the same, more than one of them felt that tiny betraying shiver up the spine. That had to be shaken off, ignored, filed away, used to stiffen their resolve.

The Argies came in sight, spread out, moving cautiously, yet lacking that feline quality that distinguished the personnel of Strike Force. Their big round helmets bobbed along, their rifles stuck up at odd angles. Yet they came on. They came on.

Barky was fully aware of his reluctance to shoot these people. That he had to do so, that he had to open fire and cut them down, was a small and ugly part of a greater and uglier whole.

The machine guns rattled death.

'The turdheads,' Deadly was saying to himself, over and over. 'The stupid sodding turdheads.'

The hostiles reacted to the fire, flinging themselves flat, crawling into whatever cover was handy – but there was previous little of that where Strike Force had them pinned down.

'Give 'em five minutes, maximum,' said Barky. 'Then we pull out. I've an itch.'

The snarling crackle of gunfire, the flat taste of burnt powder, the whine and smack of bullets all contributed to the insanity of the war. A fresh outburst of shooting from the flank where SS and Dingle were in business told Barky he'd been absolutely right. There was no need for him to use the wireless. Everyone knew that the new shooting over there meant the Argies had put out a flank force.

The instant reaction from Barky came from his training and experience, and also from that itch.

'Pull back,' he called over the set. '*Now*!'

A long stuttering burst from the jimpy scythed across the Argie positions. Then he and Deadly were packing up and squirming back between the rocks and over the crest at the back where they could stand up and belt hard down the slope.

The other teams legged it with them.

It crossed Barky's mind to halt at the next small slope and put in a few well-chosen bursts to make the hostiles believe the opposition was in depth. Tactically it was a sound move. He decided against it the instant that the first Argie mortar bombs smashed down, blowing gouts of earth and rock from the crest they'd just vacated.

It would take a minor adjustment of the sights and elevating screw to lift the tubes of the mortars onto the new target. Strike Force could be blown away the moment they opened up from the new position.

He swung his free arm vigorously. They'd keep going over the next ridge.

He did not wish to think about how long they could keep this up. They would continue to harass and delay the Argies until the job was successfully completed of course; but he felt like a man with a noose closing round his neck.

Spread out, moving with incredible speed under their burdens, they tabbed along over the rise and dipped down the reverse slope. Now they would be out of observation of the Argies when they, in their turn, crested the ridge.

They kept on going. They were small, animated dots in the desolate landscape.

Barky heard the engine note, and cursed. Up ahead, swinging up from the bowels of the ground before them, a Pucara flew up, turned, and headed directly for the exposed men of Strike Force.

CHAPTER FIVE

Punch Fuller woke up with his head as clear as a bell, his skull like Saint Paul's Cathedral, his senses alert. He was *compos mentis*, and he knew it.

He couldn't see past an odd black rectangular shape plastered before his eyes. For a heart-stopping moment he thought he'd gone blind again. Then he reached up and ripped the scrap of paper from where it had been tucked under his cap. He turned it over and read what Dexter had written.

'If I'm not back in two hours, you're on your own.'

Two hours?

That was typical of the Joker, that was.

Punch lay in the hide they'd made. So the Joker had brought him back. Punch remembered something of what had passed on the headland. He'd been firmly of the opinion that he should go up there and mallet a few Argies. Then ... then?

Yeah, that was it. The Joker had hit him. No doubt about it.

Infernal nerve! Sergeant Dexter had struck WOII Fuller. That was worthy of a court martial, that was, boy.

Punch remained lying on his back, remembering. If he

knew Dexter then he'd have gone skulking off to see what was going on on the other side of the headland. It was the obvious next move.

But two hours?

So Dexter had hit him a lick. How long had he been unconscious? He checked his watch. Not long, not with a jaw like his. And the blow must have cleared up some of the fog in his head; he felt really good now.

Punch Fuller entertained a deep respect for the Joker Dexter. He put stock in what his oppo said. Right then. He'd give him, what – hour and a half? Say hour and thirty-five minutes. Then, why then Punch Fuller would be off on his own account to sort out a few hostiles. Yes, sir!

He began to think of Sharon and the way she had of nibbling his ear at certain moments; but somehow his memories shifted to thinking about Colonel, or General, Gunjepoo. What a wally!

He did not expect to hear the Joker returning, and he'd just reached the point where they'd been tooling up for the job, at what seemed a long time ago now, when Dexter's low-voiced call reached him.

'You awake, Punch? Or you still skiving off?'

'Come in here, you great narner, Joker!'

Dexter's body slid into the hide and at once took up its allotment of space. Punch bulked in his own corner. He glared balefully at the indistinct blob of darkness that was his oppo.

'You hit me, Joker!'

'What? Me hit a big feller like you. Come off it, Punch.'

'You bleeding struck a superior officer.'

'Couldn't have. You must have fallen down, or

something. Idle on parade, more like.'

'Yeah?'

'Sure.'

'Well, me head's fine now. I feel like a million. But if you didn't hit me, I can't say thanks for that, can I?"

'You can play a tune as well as anybody.'

'Too right. I don't forget. What d'you suss out?'

Joker expelled a sharp breath of air. Both men were mere smudges of darkness in the hide. But Punch knew at once his oppo was expressing deep concern.

'Went around the other side. Barbed wire. Made a hole and got through. Shut it up all neat and tidy when I came back. Don't reckon the Argies'll spot it.'

'Check. And?'

'There are a lot of caves in that cliff face. The Argies were beavering away. Hoisting stuff up.'

'Stuff? What stuff?'

'Missiles. Looked like Exocets.'

'*Exocets*!'

'That's what the man said.'

'The cunning bastards! Well, we've got to go and mallet 'em and blow those bleeding Exocets up. That's certain.'

'Yeah. But we won't do it on our tod.'

'We can –'

'I scouted the place. Lots of bleeding Argies. Lots of wire. Mines, too, I shouldn't wonder. Better call Noggy and spell it out.'

'Well –'

'I'll call.'

Punch knew his oppo was right. But he dearly wanted to go and bash somebody to release the tension in him caused by the rough treatment he had been receiving lately.

This discovery, of ground-launched Exocets, was far too important for them to botch the job. The Exocet missile had already sunk H.M.S. *Sheffield*. The ships of the Task Force remained at risk until every blasted missile had been accounted for.

Using the big scimitar, Dexter called out to Noggy and filled him in. He spelled out the current situation, gave their present location and state of readiness. He finished, 'Those Exocets can do a lot of nasties, Noggy. Something's got to be done about 'em, and sharpish, too.'

'I agree. I'll get on to it.'

'Punch and me are ready to go in if necessary. That is, if we don't get any support real soon. Savvy, Noggy?'

'Oh, sure, Joker. I savvy what you're saying. That's vetoed for the moment. I'll get back to you.'

Dexter cut the connection and in the gloom of the hide turned to Punch.

'No doubt a considerable quantity of sweat is going to be shed over in H.M.S. *Fearless*. Yes?'

'Oh, indisputably.'

'Then it'll be *Hermes*. Then, Punch, me old china, it'll come back to descend on our noggins.'

'What I said at the start.'

Despite the stridency of his words, which rang with much hollow mockery in his ears, Dexter could see the way of it. If it had to be, it had to be. That was all there was to it.

They settled down to await the dictate of the masters on high.

There'd been an uncomfortable wait before they'd received the signal to go in the Gunjepoo Affair. That was a long time ago now and eight thousand miles away.

Two unexplained bomb outrages had taken place in London's West End. A restaurant and a night club had been blown up and gutted. Four people had died. Responsibility was not claimed by any known terrorist group.

One of the dead was a civilian, a London business man dining out. Two of the others were diplomats from Nariscia, one of the new developing countries emerging onto the world stage by virtue of undeveloped mineral and agricultural wealth and by a confused tangle of internal politics.

The men of Strike Force, heavily engaged on brutal exercises devised by Major Dan Granville to test them to the brink of stamina and willpower, more often turned to page three than studied details of more city bombings.

The fourth person to die was a pretty waitress. Her picture took the attention of Rommel, who snorted his disgust as the patrols imbibed hot tea whilst awaiting fresh Major-inspired tortures.

'Waste,' declared Rommel. 'Bloody stupid waste.'

'Let's see,' said Spider.

'Yeah,' said his oppo Lawless. 'Criminal waste. What they want to blow her up for?'

'Innocent bystander,' said Pugsy. 'They always catch it when the fan's switched on.' Then, reflectively, he added, 'Y'know, if someone blew up Jonie, or Sasha, I reckon –'

'Yeah,' cut in Trampas, tilting his wideawake back. 'We know, Pugsy. And you'd get plenty of help.'

'Too right,' growled Thwackers.

Jock, as usual, said nothing; but they all knew how he felt.

Still, this affair, unpleasant though it might be, was no

business of Strike Force. The Major ran them ragged, and all their energies had to be concentrated on keeping up to his exacting standards.

Once a bloke was fortunate enough to be asked to join Special Strike Force he'd fight tooth and nail to stay in. Too bloody right!

Then Barky clawed his way up the face of the mountain and told them to finish their chai, get their kit stowed and move on up the near-vertical cliff before he slapped them down for being idle on parade.

The newspaper folded up with the pathetic face of the pretty waitress staring out went into Rommel's pack and then he was scrambling along with the rest of them.

That face, what had happened, and the men's imaginations, merged – just for the moment – into mere words and regrets. They agreed with Rommel and Pugsy. A stupid waste, and if that happened to any of their girl friends then the evil buggers who'd done it would be sorry, very sorry ...

Snug in the hide down in the Falklands, Punch Fuller knew that his oppo the Joker Dexter was right. They just had to wait to see what the brass decided. Still and all. Like any member of Strike Force, he was capable of violent and vicious action at the right time and in the right place. He was also, again like all the SSF, capable of sitting or standing still for hours on end, just watching, observing, noting and waiting.

Sometimes he considered that Special Strike Force spent just about all its time doing the latter rather than the former. It wasn't true, of course, and the moments of violence, when they came, were with them a long, long time.

Somehow or other he started thinking of Diane, a girl

whose legs started at the floor and went, as the saying had it, up to heaven. She used to tease him pretty fiercely. She had very dark blue-black hair, cut severely across her forehead. Her eyes were sometimes hazel and sometimes green; and Punch played a great part in causing them to change colour. Yes, she'd been a good romp.

That time, just after midnight, in the Happy Days Motel when she'd thrown a slipper at him and he'd chased her, shrieking with laughter about the room until she'd dodged out through the front door. He'd followed her into a beautiful still moonlit night, and the damned door had slammed and locked after him. They'd both been starkers.

Oh, yes, that had been an interesting experience.

Dexter shifted and said grumpily: 'What the hell are you sniggering at, Punch?'

'How cheeky climbed in the window.'

'Yeah?'

Punch hadn't told this story to his oppo. Now he said: 'Sure. Fascinating sight.'

'I believe you.'

What Punch didn't say was that the local dance had turned out then. The people came out of the dance laughing and merry and that she-devil Diane stood inside the door of the chalet, teasing him. She wouldn't open the door for a long time. Punch, left stranded, hid in the bushes until the dancers departed.

When, at last, he was let in he showed cheeky Diane that his vigil outside had not chilled him at all. Quite the reverse, in fact.

And it was true, her legs did go up to heaven.

Dexter said: 'About time Noggy got it sorted.'

'Won't be Noggy, anyway.'

'No.'

About an hour after that Noggy came on the air. 'Joker? It's on. We've got the green light. All systems go.'

'About time too.'

'You'll have to wait.'

'Yeah. Just don't make it too long.'

'Wait,' said Punch, twitching himself around in the hide. 'I should have joined the cavalry.'

CHAPTER SIX

A bunch of pack-rats disappearing down their holes would have appeared slothful laggards to the men of Number Three Wing, Special Strike Force as the Pucara whined towards them.

One moment they were out in the open legging it for all they were worth; the next they were under bushes, behind rocks, flat in little depressions. Yet fast as they were, and motionless and camouflaged as they now remained, some of them were right in the path of the aircraft. Some of them couldn't escape the air strike.

In the centre of the formation, Barky and Deadly Dennis saw they were in for it.

'Sod this for a game of chess,' said Barky.

He and Deadly had tumbled into a bush. There was no time to think. Time only to act, and act at once.

Deadly bent forward, shoulders broad, and Barky slammed the jimpy on this improvised rest. He barely aimed. He saw the oncoming wings and blob of fuselage, lined up and let fly. He pressed the trigger and kept it pressed as the machine gun bucked and leaped on Deadly's shoulder and he slammed the rounds out, hosing down the incoming aircraft.

Over on the flank SS and Dingle joined in the

fusillade. Others added their fire. In an instant five machine guns were spitting and belching flame and lead at the Pucara.

Strikes scored along the wing and an engine. The pilot, like most of the Argentinian pilots, was a brave man. He bored on. Some vital part of the controls must have been hit in the torrent of fire for the plane slewed. In the instant the bomb dropped free the plane skidded. It righted itself at once under the pilot's skilful hands, but the bombs flew wide.

The nose-level of the aircraft prevented forward fire. The five jimpys followed the plane around, scything lead and fear-filled hatred. The Pucara flew on.

No need for instructions on the drill now. In the time it would take for the twin-engined aircraft to bank and turn back, Strike Force upped sticks and, selecting better holes, vanished once again into the featureless landscape.

The Pucara buzzed back, her yellow identification stripe bright, her propellers silver discs. She flew over and then turned again. The men of Strike Force barely breathed.

An odd clicketty-clacketty note sounded in the even roar of the aircraft's engines. Barky perked up instantly. His view of the plane through a tiny gap along the edge of the poncho revealed her as circling around again. She vanished from his view.

Deadly said: 'Persistent bugger.'

'Listen,' said Barky.

The intermittent interruption in the steady sound of the engines increased in frequency. Barky saw the Pucara turning one more time and then the uneven engine note dwindled. When it had faded, he started to count.

He gave the persistent beast five hundred counts.

Then, over the wireless, he called out, 'Any sign?'
No one replied.
'Check.' He pondered a moment, and then said: 'If the Argies had followed up as they've been doing they'd be here by now.'
He waited. No one responded.
'Right. Move out. And we don't *know* they've given up. That remains speculation.'
As they started off Deadly remarked, 'The good Lord has seen fit to strike the hostiles with doubt, I reckon. Won't see them again.'
'I devoutly trust so. Now hack it!'
The shattering explosions of the bombs the plane had dropped off target persisted in Barky's head. That had been an experience he did not wish to repeat.
Hacking along Barky knew that the British soldier's habit of making a joke of everything, of finding amusement in the most grisly circumstances contributed to his sanity and to his capacity to deal with the many horrifying incidents that fate handed him.
They were well down on ammunition for the machine guns and their lightened loads barely hindered progress so that they made a cracking pace. The weather remained clear and sharp and the infernal wind blew mournfully about their ears.
Continuous checking of the backtrail revealed no sign of pursuit.
After a time Barky, as commander, began to allow himself furtive thoughts of halting for a brew up. The Argies must have given up the chase, at least on foot, though no doubt more aircraft and helicopters would come buzzing and nosing about to find them.
When, at last, he gave the order to halt they'd put a

few miles between themselves and their last hostile encounter. With their usual ability to make something out of near-nothing, they built tidy little hides, settled in and started a brew up.

There were at least two reasons for this. One was obvious: if the Argentine Air Force came looking for them they'd be invisible. Two: they couldn't be absolutely sure the Argie soldiers had given up the pursuit. Therefore they built themselves sound defensive positions.

Shrimp had caught the duty of lugging the big scimitar along. Barky had commented urbanely that as Shrimp had been serving as communications guru at HQ he was clearly more highly qualified for the job in the field. Shrimp, his heavy moustache not exactly dropping but spiking upwards far less arrogantly than those of the others, harrumphed at this logic, but took the job with the same determination that they all possessed to do whatever job they were handed to the best of their ability.

He called out for Noggy, and Barky took the handset.

'Noggy? We've had a little fun and games. In the clear at the moment.'

The situation was laid out. Barky was anticipating no more than that they should continue with the operation. He felt interested surprise as Noggy corrected that view.

'You're to pull out at once, Barky. Transport is laid on. Make it quick and quiet.'

'Check. But we're not really finito here.'

'Oh yes you are.'

Barky jotted down the co-ordinates for the pick up and the timing. Deadly Dennis lay back on his elbows beaming.

'The Good Lord has arranged more mischief for us. I feel it in my bones.'

'Don't tell me what you feel in your water.'

Noggy finished up, 'And, Barky, you'll have to hack it sharpish. Got it?'

'Got it.'

Roller's yell ripped in at that moment. 'Chopper.'

A heartbeat later Barky heard the helicopter engine. He was confident the Argentinian observer scudding along up there wouldn't spot Strike Force. If he had IR equipment, the story would be different, of course.

Under close scrutiny from the British hidden on the ground below, the Argentinian helicopter chip-chop-chipped by above. She flew a neat mathematical course, carrying out a close sweep. You had to hand it to the Argie fly boys. They were no slouches when it came to flying.

Deadly was itching to have a crack. Barky vetoed the idea, and they sat tight and watched silently and unmoved until the heli chattered away.

'What's up, anyway, Barky?' Roller wanted to know.

'Emergency op. That's all I know. The blue light's gone up somewhere.'

'Bunch of wallies in it up to their armpits, I expect.'

'Yeah.'

'They shall not call upon the Lord in vain,' said Deadly, 'when we get the word.'

'Kit up and move out,' said Barky. 'Stretch them legs. *Move*!'

There was, of course, absolutely no need for him to say unnecessary things like that. Deadly cocked a quick concerned eye at him. Barky well knew what Deadly Dennis was worrying about in that complex brain of his.

Yes, Barky was well aware he could fall into a fit of depression. But he usually knew why. When he didn't was the time to become concerned.

Strike Force moved out. They might move along like a pack of savage hunting animals; they were not animals, they were trained soldiers doing their job. If their *esprit de corps* was such that they believed themselves to be the best force there was, they couldn't be faulted for that. Plenty of outfits believed themselves to be the best. It was all part of the system.

When they'd been tasked with sorting out the Gunjepoo problem, for instance, they perfectly understood they'd been selected because they were the best.

Major Dan Granville's dark red hair had sparkled as he sat at the wooden table in the nondescript hut they currently called HQ. He slammed his stick down with a bang.

'We're out on our own on this one,' he had told the assembly. They all sat or stood silently, alert, waiting, taking it all in. Not one of them failed to understand the feelings the Old Man had for his creation, Special Strike Force. He had selected them all personally, with the exception of Captain Tom Burnaby, who fitted in perfectly with the force. What the Major said was Gospel. They'd follow him anywhere.

Most of them were stripped to the waist for the sunshine poured golden and hot upon the land. The Major had condescended to strip to a shirt. He still looked as though he could organise, command and control the Queen's Birthday Parade without effort.

'The feller's called Gunjepoo. His real name is

unpronounceable, more or less. So that's what he's been called. He's a colonel, and he calls himself a general.'

'Is he the bad egg, Major,' Captain Guy Wheaton wanted to know, 'or the other side?'

'That's the rub, Guy. They're *all* bad eggs.'

'Ah!'

The Major's reddish eyebrows bristled up. His eyes of that curious pale grey bored through a fellow like twin Toledo blades. He'd created Special Strike Force. He was absolutely confident it was an instrument that would not fail.

'We've been selected because we are a newish formation and we are, unlike some other top line forces, completely unknown.'

'How does that figure, Major?' said Lieutenant Christopher Smythe-Jones.

'Figure, Smyjo?' The Major was not above a gentle cutting remark or three. 'You've been watching romantic films, my boy, I am certain.'

Smyjo, the SSF's Intelligence Officer, a big, bulky, deadly man who pre-eminently demonstrated among them all their own special martial art of keninja, did not rise to the bait.

'If –' he began.

'The point is,' interrupted the Old Man. 'We are faced with a covert op here. If the world media in any way come across this story, we are on our own.'

Barky, with his police training, was not the only one among them moved to remark that they were British soldiers, and dark and desperate undercover operations weren't quite their cup of tea.

The Major bridled at this.

'Listen, all of you, and listen out well. Yes, we are

British soldiers, and damned proud of that, too! Now we are faced with a situation where the government cannot be seen to be interfering with the internal politics of a fringe country. God knows which way they'll jump.'

Smyjo said, 'I rather gather they have a strong Marxist faction, coupled with a Stalinist rump, where multi-national conglomerates are out to stake various claims, and the indigenous population crave for Japanese Tvs and videos and cameras and cars rather than little red books. But, as you rightly say, Major, they can jump any way.'

'As I said, the folk struggling for control at the moment are all bad eggs from the point of view of their neighbouring countries. If one faction is able to take over completely and control the whole country, one or other of the neighbours are highly likely to invade and attempt to take over.'

'That will not be good,' said Guy.

'Too damned right it won't be good! It'll rupture the whole structural balance. Oh, no, not only our government will sweat blood if that happens.'

'And,' put in Barky, sticking to the point that bothered him. 'They are killing and blowing one another up over here.'

'Murdering British citizens in the process. Yes.'

'So,' summed up Lieutenant Charlie Mainwaring, Strike Force's Quartermaster, 'We go in and do the job and if something happens to create a stench, the government have no knowledge whatsoever of our existence.'

'Complete disavowal,' confirmed the Major. 'The

government have never heard of us. We don't officially exist.'

'Nice,' said a deep voice from the rear of the hut.

'Yeah,' rapped out the Old Man, sharply. 'Yeah. Nice. That means we do the job in our own way. No interference.'

'Provided,' Smyjo had to say, 'we keep it low key.'

'You mean not more than one four-letter word a page of script?' The remark, a jibe though it was, from Sergeant-Major Andrew Stubbs, hit the nail on the head. That, more or less, was how it would be. Strike Force could wade in shooting and if nothing too drastic occurred they'd get away with it. If innocent bystanders were involved – well, there would be a number of vacant chairs in the London Clubs, and the NAAFI in certain areas would be missing some of its valued customers.

'Y'know,' said Noggy, and he pulled the lobe of his right ear reflectively. 'These blasted countries with their diabolical internal foul-ups. We're bad enough here in Britain; but as far as I know we don't go around machine gunning one another and blowing MP's up outside the Houses of Parliament. I wish some of these sodding fringe countries would grow up.'

'It took some time before the English settled down to some responsible government, Noggy,' said the Major. He did not speak in a reproving tone of voice; the sentiment was unmistakable.

'Yeah,' said Guy. 'These poor benighted sods have a long way to go before they can accept proper forms of government.'

Although they weren't thinking of Argentina at the time, considered Barky as he hacked on rapidly across the bleak and featureless Falklands landscape, the wind blowing about him, had they known what the future held they might well have included that unhappy land in their strictures.

CHAPTER SEVEN

'Hack and slay,' said Punch. 'That's the way to do it. Why, up on the Borders they were always at it.'

'Yeah,' said Dexter. 'They fought each other and they fought anyone else who came along. Charming.'

'Oh, I dunno. Three hundred years or so they had at it. Peel towers, being bashed, raids, forays, rustling, ransoms. What a life!'

'Well, there's precious little up there now, apart from grouse moors.'

'Some people call shooting birds and animals sport.'

'Well, the Argies are going to have sport shooting their Exocets at our ships across the water if we don't stop 'em sharpish.'

'We will. We will.'

'Yeah.'

They relapsed into silence in the hide. Each one's thoughts dwelt darkly on what lay ahead, and then drifted off to happier times.

Punch heard the tiny rattle of stones outside. He could see nothing in the dimness. He didn't bother to haul up the night sight and take a dekko. He knew who was there homing in on the wireless directions.

'Like a herd of bleeding elephants,' his voice growled

into the darkness. 'Makes me think you must be Argies.'

Barky's voice floated in with that delicate balance of distance and whisper combined. 'We've got enough stuff here to blow up Fort Knox.'

'Fat lot of good that'd be. They don't keep the gold there anymore, do they?'

The newcomers moved in and prepared their own hides. Dexter wanted a word with Barky. That had been a typical new-style Punch there, jabbering away about Fort Knox – Good grief! – and it might have to come down to Lieutenants telling Warrant Officers what to do. Dexter wanted Punch out of it and safely in the S.S. *Uganda* where they could survey, map out and possibly dismantle his skull.

'Not,' said Dexter to himself in a fine surly manner, 'they'd find owt there.'

There was too little time left that night for the operation to take place. Their very own launch from the drab little HQ ship had lifted them off from East Falkland. They'd had time for a few hours kip, most of it on passage, and they'd rekitted with large amounts of plastic and fresh ammunition. The five jimpys had been returned to store from whence, no doubt, some eager-beaver ordnance officer would press them into valuable service ashore on the islands.

'Lot of ships in the Sound and San Carlos Water,' said Barky. 'If these Argies here set up their damned Exocets ... Be like fish in a barrel. No distance at all for the missile.'

'They're in holes in the cliff, sort of caves,' pointed out Dexter. 'The fly boys have no chance at all of knocking them out.'

'Quite.'

'So we take all this lovely bangum-powder,' said Punch. 'And send 'em sky high.'

Dexter felt the muscle at the side of his mouth twitch. Poor old Punch really ought to be seen to. The Joker might have failed to get Punch sent off so far; that didn't mean he'd stop trying.

The difference between the loose-lipped Punch Fuller of today and the taciturn Punch Fuller of the time they'd been engaged on the Gunjepoo caper seemed to Dexter alarming and frightening. Barky just had to be made to see reason.

Number Three Wing Special Strike Force spent the next day with heads down in their hides, completely invisible. Sentries were posted. They took the opportunity to catch up on lost sleep and to prepare weapons and explosives. They'd go in light, and all of them would go.

When Dexter managed to get Barky to himself for a few moments, Barky was unconvinced.

'Yeah, Punch is chattering away like a parrot, I know. But you can see the knock on the head hasn't affected his fighting ability, Joker. He's still –'

'Yeah! He can still fight all right. But, Barky –'

'He's far too valuable to be left out. Anyway, d'you think he'd stay here when we go in?'

Dexter bit his lip. 'No.'

'Well, then.'

'Just that he isn't himself.'

Barky felt for the Joker. It was apparent he believed Punch to be still suffering from the effects of his injury to the extent that he was in peril. Barky didn't see it in that light. Sure, Punch wasn't quite the tight-lipped Punch of yore. But maybe the circumstances of being on active duty down here in the South Atlantic caused that.

'You said yourself he's acting completely naturally, apart from talking, and he's performing well. His blindness has not recurred. His head doesn't hurt. No, Joker. Punch is –'

'Yeah. Punch is Punch, one of the very best.' Dexter was about to go on and say something like, 'I just hope nothing dire happens and he gets knocked off.' But he checked himself. Recriminations ahead of time wouldn't help the situation and might well make it worse.

The planners ought to have felt that, too. So far, despite the inevitable chaos accompanying any operation of war, the planners had done well. They'd gathered a fleet, a fleet train and transports together, organised troops and stores, and sent the whole lot across eight thousand miles of ocean with only a halfway stop at Ascension. All that had been done in an incredibly short time.

They'd successfully put ashore a Commando Brigade strengthened by two Parachute Battalions. These formations were supported by all arms. Armour was there in the shape of the Scorpions and Scimitars of the Blues and Royals.

And, in doing this, the Royal Navy had lost warships. The ferociousness and fury of the Argentinian air attacks demanded an accolade of bravery from their opponents. The Argie flyboys had guts. Plenty of them. And with the deadliness of the air attacks scourging the ships in San Carlos Water the gunline really didn't need the further attentions of Exocets.

Barky, like them all, knew the seriousness of the situation.

Also, he knew the Argie positions were very strongly

defended. Dexter's report was precise and specific. There was wire, mines were no doubt strewn about everywhere, machine guns would criss-cross the area, mortars would have the ranges chalked down to centimetres. By the time Strike Force got through that series of obstacles and gunfire they'd find the Argie soldiery who'd shoot them up with glee.

The precision of Dexter's report might pinpoint machine guns and wire; in the nature of the beast it could only indicate mined areas. Barky mulled it all over in that wispily-clad skull of his. The more he thought about it, the less he liked it. Strike Force could be mangled on this one. Number Three Wing could cease to exist.

The job had to be done, for the sake of the men out there in the Sound and across on East Falkland.

Barky was fond of remembering his pre-SSF life, often saying: 'Now if I'd carried on my career with the Police Force I'd never be in this mess,' and then go on to categorise the particular mucky position in which he found himself. He'd have made sergeant, possibly inspector, by now. Be a detective. On the narcotics or vice squad, perhaps got a transfer to Special Branch or the Sweeney. Yeah. And maybe he'd still be a copper directing the traffic.

That was another world, along with hang-gliding and fast cars and pretty girls. Major Dan Granville had trained up Special Strike Force to do what it set out to do.

This time wouldn't be any different.

The personnel of SSF regarded the Old Man as the source of all wisdom. What the Major said was gospel. Now he'd been wounded and was out of the fight. Barky felt the loss keenly. Captain Tom Burnaby had spoken to Barky in the most veiled terms, the drift of which was that Tom was not altogether convinced that this cult of personality was altogether a 'Good Thing' for Strike Force.

If Tom Burnaby expected Strike Force to fall to pieces with the departure of the Major, then, so Barky reckoned, Tom was on a non-starter. Barky knew very little about what had happened to Number One Wing over there on the mainland. They'd done the job. Now they were swanning about with the invasion, doing nasties to Argies on East Falkland, and helping in the eventual drive on Port Stanley.

Still and all, wouldn't it be marvellous to have the Major with them now!

Barky could see him now, reddish eyebrows bristling, those slatey-steel eyes surveying everything and that incisive brain knowing exactly what to do about everything. The foreshortened brim of the Old Man's cap told you from whence he hailed. Oh, yes, he was a right hellion on wheels, Major Dan Granville.

And his own personal firearm! Weird, that was. On a Lee-Enfield rifle a .45 calibre barrel and magazine housing had been fitted. The thing had a dubiously short range, only around two hundred and fifty metres or so. But the gimmick was the silencer, a series of discs so arranged that the gases from the cartridge explosion could trundle around and lose their energy and noise before being squirted out through holes in the casing. Some bloke called de Lisle had invented this wonderful piece back in the war for Commandos to use. It had worked splendidly; but D-Day and the drive across France had reduced the need for its services, and stocks of the piece had been sent out to the Far East where they'd mostly disappeared after use in the Malayan Emergency.

As a quondam police officer, Barky could see the potential danger they posed as assassination weapons.

Captain Tom Burnaby had voiced his own personal uneasiness about the Major's policy of allowing each man in Strike Force to choose his own personal weapon.

One beneficial result from Burnaby's point of view was that he'd been able to kit his signals group with the new Enfield Weapons System firearms. Barky quite liked the Enfield IW and the machine gun version, the LSW. Burnaby had left a rather sharp, not to say caustic, note to the effect that he wanted to see greater uniformity at least in ammunition calibres in future patrols.

With him now Barky had three calibres; the 7.62 mm NATO rifle cartridge, the 9 mm SMG round and the 5.56 mm sub-calibre for the Armalites and EIWs. Some changing around had taken place regarding weapons when they'd kitted for this bothersome job against these Exocets. All the same, SS had hung onto his Heckler und Koch HK33 like grim death.

Considering the future, Barky conceded he had plenty of firepower. He had vast quantities of C3, looking and smelling like marzipan. He had the men. He also had the resolve. Just that, well, he knew damn well he was not looking forward to this particular op.

Of one thing he was absolutely, nauseatingly assured. There'd be mines. He detested mines. Well, any sane person would. Unless, of course, you were using them to protect your own positions.

Briefing indicated the Argies had a wide variety of unpleasant mines at their disposal, obtained from a number of sources. Apart from the anti-tank mines of American origin and World War II vintage, there were modern plastic examples.

As Barky and his men would not be driving up in a Chieftain or a Challenger, not even in a Scorpion or a Scimitar, the anti-tank mines, unless the detonating pressure was very light indeed, should not inconvenience them overmuch. It was the damned anti-personnel mines that put the heebie-jeebies up a fellow.

Here the Argies could deploy Israeli, Spanish and Italian examples of effective man-maiming and man-killing devices. Nasty.

He thrust these unpleasant thoughts out of this mind, for what needed to be done about mines would be done when they went in. He checked his camouflage cream, although his face was grimy enough in all conscience by now. The men in Strike Force used camouflage creams of different colours, of course, and the Major had settled on a lighter green and a dullish ochre. By the time white and black were war-painted up there was little difference to choose in their appearance.

The teams and patrols had been assigned their various tasks. Barky checked his watch. Not long now.

Naturally enough, Punch had insisted on getting stuck in right up front. Because he was indisputably an invaluable member of the unit, he took that task from Barky, his craggy lips splitting into a satisfied smile.

Aware though he was of Dexter's concerns over Punch, Barky felt far more confidence in the big fellow than he had earlier on. He'd been given a clean bill of health, his skull intact and wits all there. The main problem was his tendency to talk and jabber away all the time, and this was something the doctors felt was at least for the moment outside their sphere. When it came down to action, Punch Fuller was his old grim and scythe-wielding self.

Everything was set for the off.
Barky checked his watch.
He heaved up and flipped out the scimitar. His words were calm and level.
'Right. Let's get moving.'

CHAPTER EIGHT

One of the problems for Barky, as the commander of the force, was that he couldn't be everywhere at once.

He had to decide where he was going to be, let everyone know, and then pass on the location of any subsequent moves he made. He certainly did not intend to stick in one spot all the time.

Weather conditions were reasonable, not ideal, with the wind dropping away and not really enough of a mist to conceal their activities. There was just enough light to pick out objects but with Strike Force intending to be on the move all the time the night sight problem ought to be minimised.

Stripped down to battle kit, Barky moved rapidly along the shoreline heading for the Argie positions. He breathed evenly. He could feel the blood thumping around his body; but that was not unusual – it meant the was scared right down to his socks. That was normal too, and he knew his fear would vanish once the fireworks started.

He and the other lads used that kind of euphemism from time to time. They weren't trying to shut their eyes to what lay ahead by double-talk. If they killed someone they killed them. Yet sometimes they said they would mallet them. The words conveyed far more than the letters composing them.

Timing would prove critical.

Sniper and Huey were up on the headland, moving in to make a demonstration of firepower, explosions and general uproar. They'd start the action when the second hands of their watches reached zero hour. By that time Punch and his party should be in position, and Barky and his lot also should be ready for the final penetration.

The night breathed round him. He felt good. His body, freed from the gargantuan weights it normally hefted about the islands, responded. For an odd silly second Barky felt he could soar up and do a spot of hang-gliding without a glider at all.

When he returned there would be even less to carry. The C3 would have been expended. That would be another good thing; they could well be in a devil of a hurry when they passed this way again.

The sea on one side, the cliff on the other, the teams prowled on in the semi-darkness.

In theory the Argentinians marked their minefields with a single strand of wire on the inner side, using a panel system. Up front, Punch and Dexter, now crawling along, checked constantly. They had mine probes in their fists and their faces were taut and intent.

They could see no signs of wire that might indicate the edge of a mine panel, but only barbed wire strung on posts, stretching from the waves to the cliff face. The cliff was not vertical and was pierced at various levels by the shadowy openings of caves.

Cautiously, Punch inched forward, his extended fingers feeling through the gritty sand. If the Argies wanted to set up a trip wire and booby trap they had at their disposal the Israeli Number Four anti-personnel mine. This was a box type, fitted with push or pull switches. It was very nasty.

Punch and Dexter eased forward very carefully. Yet they made good progress. SS and Dingle followed up, double-checking the edges of the cleared path.

Bringing up the rear, abaft Barky's patrol, Bunce and Chunky had been entrusted with most of the explosives. They were burdened more than the others, and they had to put their trust completely in the efficiency of those in front who cleared the way.

There was absolutely no point in feeling all tensed up and jumpy. Nerves had to be used. You had to let yourself feel as one with the night, with the susurration of the sea, the chill of the air, the smell of weeds and damp rocks, of grit and sweat and oily mechanism.

Just as he was about to convince himself there were no mines, Punch discovered the first. He breathed in and out. With exquisite care he removed the offending object. It was not booby-trapped. He moved on.

The barbed wire ahead seemed to stay where it was for ever. For every foot of progress made, the wire seemed to come closer only inches.

Punch and Dexter stuck grimly to their task. Now they were brains, muscles and eyes, their fingers more sensitive than those of a surgeon. Slowly, cautiously and safely, they opened the way.

Some mines had to be left in situ. These were marked. There was enough light for them not to have to work in completely pitch darkness. SS and Dingle widened the path. Barky and the rest followed on.

No thought entered Punch's or Dexter's minds – or those of any of the others, come to that – of their mangled bodies sprawled out, their guts blown inside out, their private portions missing, their arms and legs scattered. Every cell of their bodies had to concentrate on the task in hand. Anything less would not be tolerated, might be lethal. And the inescapable fact remained: one mistake could result in horrific maiming or hideous death.

At last – at long bloody last – they reached the barbed wire.

It was quite different this time from the occasion on the headland for Punch and Dexter. They checked everything with minute care. The tins of stones could be dealt with. Wires to pull the pins on grenades or to detonate booby traps could be immunised. They brought out the wire cutters and started to work. SS and Dingle joined them.

Occasional sounds of mechanical activity reached them from further along the beach and cliff. No real illumination along there revealed much of what was going on, but there were a few scattered lights, here and there. Whatever was happening – and the Brits could guess what that was easily enough – was taking place at night to avoid interruption and sudden death at the efficient hands of the Harriers.

The sliding gritty sounds of footsteps sent everyone's heads down. Narrowed eyes regarded the sentry as he slouched past, rifle slung, helmet tipped. At least he was not smoking a cigarette. Cigarettes were death to a soldier in more ways than one.

When he'd passed Punch breathed into Dexter's ear.

'Next time, Joker, and we mallet him.'

Dexter did not reply.

Instead he checked his watch. He thrust the dial under

Punch's nose. The big fellow squinted down at it.

'Yeah. Couple more minutes.'

The last strand of wire parted. Punch lifted up slightly and eased forward. Dexter squirmed along. He didn't follow Punch but wriggled forward at his side. As before, they might need a wider gap on the return trip.

Above their heads the uncut wire drooped ready to stick the barbs into them. From aloft, no doubt, the wire looked all right. If the sentry spotted a few gaps where strands might be expected to stretch, he looked dozy enough to shrug and drift on, dreaming of *senôritas* and good food and a few drinks with the *caballeros*.

Once through the wire, they trusted, they sincerely trusted they'd run into no further mines.

For a fellow who wanted his inner parts to remain inside him, who didn't much fancy having his arms and legs sent flying every which way, any close acquaintanceship with mines was anathema.

Inside the wire they fanned out. Each of them knew what his assignment was. Because, in the Joker's earlier reconnaissance he'd been unable to pinpoint every object, they weren't absolutely sure where everything was. They knew what to do once they'd found the targets.

Piled stores, some sheeted, stood about here and there. Further along men were working, humping burdens, shouting now and again as something didn't go right. The noise of the machinery increased. They had petrol engines up there, no doubt powering winches.

The sentry walked back, not really looking where he was going, and Punch had the mortification of having to allow Shrimp to clobber the fellow. Shrimp didn't mess about. The sentry was gagged, his ankles bound and his thumbs tied together. Strike Force lifted him and carried him a little way to dump him down in the lee of a pile of packing crates. They judged they ought to be well in action by the time he was missed, and probably on their way out before he was discovered.

Rommel and Woody cut off to the edge of the sea to check out the indistinct bulks beached there like stranded whales. Barges or small lighters, they'd all have charges fixed to their bottoms.

Peering out from the corner of a pile of drums, Barky gave his watch a quick check.

Yes. About now ... Up on the headland the fireworks erupted.

Huey and Sniper worked like demented beavers. Between them they let off firepower and flowering geysers of flame which might be considered to originate from a force of at least platoon strength. The bangs went on and on. They kept on shifting cover, never keeping still, slamming the stuff away.

'Luvverly,' said Punch.

'You great wally,' said Dexter. 'Over there. Looks like a ladder.'

'More'n one,' cut in SS.

'Yeah,' said Dingle. 'Up to them caves.'

'Let's see, then,' growled Punch, and led off.

On Barky's axis of advance lay what he considered to be the object of the exercise.

The hostiles were running about in all directions. The uproar they created, whilst obviously being splendid, served admirably to cloak any little chink of sound made by Strike Force. Strike Force was composed of men used to moving about silently. Like grey wolves slipping lethally among a flock of sheep, they moved towards their objectives.

The noise and confusion blossoming all about was now great enough for Dexter to stop worrying about Punch chattering on. No one was going to hear the big fellow in this lot.

'They've got launchers in them there caves.'

'Yeah.'

'The missiles come in and they winch 'em up.'

'Right. And they can only have just started, otherwise they'd have been blowing our ships to kingdom come already.'

'Already,' said Punch, making Dexter's harsh lips twitch. The big plug-ugly fellow was really all right, then.

'Get the lot,' Punch went on. 'The whole bloody shebang.'

'Up the ladders,' said SS.

'Nice,' said Dingle.

'Me and the Joker,' Punch rapped out. 'You two –'

SS yelped his outrage. 'What? Keep you covered? That's a load of old rubbish if ever I heard it!'

'Yeah,' amplified Dingle. 'What the hell could we do stuck down here?'

'Shoot the buggers, that's what. No argument. See?'

SS and Dingle turned to glare furiously back down the beach. Quickly-glimpsed figures flitted about. Lights spattered and spangled. The misshapen lumps of piles of stores seemed mere blots in the dimness. The Argentinians had been in the middle of shifting the stores up to the safety of the caves away from prying eyes. Now, with Huey and Sniper playing merry hell, everything had come to a standstill.

'Over there,' said SS, and his voice was a single surly snarl.

A group of hostiles was climbing a ladder further along. They were going up smartly enough, arms and legs working convulsively, rifles sticking out, heads tucked in. Dexter took another careful look at those Argie heads.

He could not see a single big round helmet among them.

He pointed out this fact to his comrades. They had also spotted that fascinating item of information.

'So all right, then,' said Punch. 'It's Argie Special Forces. So they're quick on the trigger. We just shoot faster, that's all.'

It wasn't all, and they knew it. But it would do to be going on with.

Dexter did not like the little shiver that went whizzing up and down his spine. Reluctantly, he said, 'I wonder if that creep Hector Caldeiro's over there?'

'If he is, me old Joker, and we run into him, I'll mallet him for what he did to you.'

'Yeah.'

Dexter would never forget his imprisonment by Captain Hector Caldeiro, an Intelligence Officer, and whilst he had no belief in the merits of revenge, he knew that daisies growing on Caldeiro's grave would be performing a valuable service to humanity.

No doubt the fact that he had swiped Caldeiro's fancy blue blazer, boots and anorak might cause the Argentinian Special Forces officer to wish to meet him again. Those objects had been left in the HQ ship when Dexter had re-kitted. One thing was for sure; if ever Fate threw Caldeiro and Strike Force together again it would be *guerre a l'outrance* with a vengeance.

Wasting no further time, Punch went up the first

ladder. Dexter followed at speed and tumbled over the lip of the cave on Punch's heels.

A single comprehensive glance showed the two that the Argies had finished their work here and had set up shop for the morrow.

Two launchers bulked like spaceship ramps in a galactic star cruiser, with the missiles lined up and ready to go. But those Exocets were no models of fantasy; they were hard and cold and waiting – and lethal.

Two Argentinian soldiers trundled around the end of the nearest launcher, arguing heatedly. They were both smoking cigarettes. They saw the two Britons just as Punch and Dexter mounted the lip of the cave.

Give the Argies their due. They went for their weapons. They carried their SMGs slung over their shoulders, and they seemed to convulse and twitch as they shrugged the slings off, grabbing for the tommies.

Punch's Patchett Sterling began firing: pop-pop! pop-pop ... The two hostiles fell.

'Silly Sods.' Punch breathed out. 'Pity, though.'

'Yeah.'

They walked warily across the littered and uneven floor of the cave. The two men sprawled, limp, dead. Punch wasted no more time or sympathy. He started to dig out the plastic.

Dexter couldn't help a flash of memory, the Major warning them that the consequences of this misunderstanding with Argentina wouldn't end when the British reclaimed the Falkland Islands. After that would come the reckoning. Well these two poor devils were dead because certain fascist hoodlums couldn't keep their cotton-picking hands off other peoples' property. Shame, really.

Dexter went to work fixing up his explosives to blow the Exocets to oblivion.

Barky's plan hinged on contingencies. He'd given time markers for certain things to happen. Huey and Sniper had been spot on, and the main body had been through the mines and the wire on time. Now Dexter and Punch set the timers to the second time marker.

If Strike Force had not completed its work by then ... Well, the ensuing confusion might give them the chance of a successful break back. At least, that was the theory.

Punch shoved the flap back over the plastic satchel. Oddly enough, given his new garrulousness, he did not say anything. He walked across to the cave mouth, dropped to his knees and stretched out. Very cautiously he stuck his head over and checked what was going on outside.

The pandemonium outside persisted. Exactly what was going on along the beach was difficult to discern. There was a great deal of shouting and yelling. Flashlights danced everywhere. A few rifleshots blasted the night air; Punch hoped these were being shot at phantoms of the imagination, shadows in the Argies' eyes, rather than at his comrades.

If Barky's plan was adhered to, the lighters or barges, or whatever the Argies' water transport was along the shoreline, should blow up next.

Further along the cliff face a machine gun opened up. The heavy clattering racket told Punch the weapon was an American Browning point fifty. It could cut a man in half.

He angled his field of vision parallel with the cliff, but could see only a long livid tongue of flame. If the Argie gunner had a target for his big fifty calibre rounds someone was in trouble. Again, Punch hoped it was not a comrade. He wished with a dark and vengeful glee that the Argies were shooting at their own people.

'Time to go, Punch.'

'Yeah. Hell of a sight out there.'

'Rommel's due next.'

'If he's on time.'

'Well, you know Rommel.'

Yes, well, they all knew Rommel. Derek Anthony Kershaw, Sergeant, was from the Tanks rather than the Infantry. He was keen, alert, tough, aggressive: all essential qualities that those in Strike Force had to possess just to be considered for selection for so august a body of troops. But, always, that curious little doubt about Rommel persisted in the minds of his comrades. Odd, that, really.

Punch put his leg over the lip of the cave mouth, swung agilely onto the ladder and started climbing down. Dexter crawled across, keeping low, and stuck his head out to take a looksee. The place was jumping like Slattery Sally's on pay night.

The detonation of a grenade punched through the din. The fifty calibre Browning went on shooting. One of the lads of Strike Force must have put a grenade in where it would do some good. The blast briefly outlined piles of tarpaulined stores the Argies desperately needed carted up the beach and into the caves before daylight.

The scything blast of the big machine gun swept around, the tongue of flame reaching out accusingly across the beach. The gunner didn't seem to care much what he hit just so long as he could keep his finger clamped on the trigger. Maybe he was in stasis and couldn't let go. Such behaviour under combat conditions was quite well known.

Halfway down the ladder Punch looked up. 'Come on, you great wally!'

'I'm coming, I'm coming.'

Dexter wriggled around and cocked a leg out, feeling for the first rung. The ladder was a solid enough affair, made from varnished wood. The rungs felt hard and round under his gloved fingers. He raked his boots onto the ladder. These were his spare pair – broken in, supple, watertight and comfortable. Pity about his first pair, taken by that bastard Captain Hector Caldeiro. Still, he'd had his off him.

Punch was two-thirds of the way down now. Dexter started down. He heard a shrill gabble of Spanish floating up and looked down under his upstretched arm.

A rattle of SMG fire broke viciously against the cliff face. He could see spurts of fire flashing up at him. Punch gave a yell and dropped the rest of the way down, going into free fall.

Stranded on the ladder, Dexter heard and saw the line of pock marks gouging into the cliff. In mere heartbeats the lethal line of machine gun bullets would scythe across his helpless body.

CHAPTER NINE

For Lieutenant Miles Barker this mission, which he had viewed with depressing dissatisfaction, was turning out quite well. Huey and Sniper up on the headland were creating merry hell and the Argies down here were running about like headless chickens. With Punch and his patrol about to kick seven kinds of brickdust out of the hostiles, Barky was happy to race ahead and get stuck in.

He did not have a great deal of time. Rommel was due to blow the lighters at the water's edge, and Barky wanted to take full opportunity of the resulting additional confusion when that happened.

Some fool hostiles were shooting. Their shots must be wild, Barky reckoned, for he couldn't see Punch and his mob exposing themselves in order to make targets for Argies Rifle and sub-machine gun fire sputtered out spasmodically. The hostiles were evidently not a happy band of invaders.

Any attempt to carry on shifting the stores up from the beach to the winches at the foot of the cliffs had been abandoned. The enemy were far too preoccupied with finding out what was going on above them and taking care of their own hides. Barky didn't blame them for that one little bit.

Deadly moved up alongside. He made an angry gesture towards the cliffs. 'Reckon they've shifted a good few of the infernal things.'

'Yeah. Can you see any lying about spare?'

Among the piles of supplies littering the beach there was, as far as Barky could ascertain, no sign of a single Exocet. Just how long the Argies had had at hauling the missiles up to their hiding places he did not know; he fancied there were more than one or two up there already.

'Quick sweep across the beach and then up to the caves.' He rapped out the command as though it had already happened. He felt good; he didn't want to lose that feeling.

'Check. And may the Good Lord have mercy on their miserable misbegotten little souls.'

Fanning out, the men of Barky's patrol stalked along the beach.

At a likely looking pile of boxes, Deadly stopped and said, 'Hold on a tic.'

Roller cut in, 'I'll take that lot over there.' He didn't think in quite the fashion of: I'm not letting Deadly get away with blowing everything up himself. There are limits. But he did think that he ought to take a hand in blowing things up. Deadly was almost as bad as the Whizz Kid at that game.

By this time the Argies ought to have responded to the turmoil on the headland. They would want to take very special care of their valuable Exocets. Quickly glimpsed figures darting away ahead drew Barky to a halt. They weren't Brits. Deadly snouted his weapon up.

'Hold it, Deadly!'

The running figures vanished past the edge of a dropped crate and vanished.

'Yeah,' said Deadly Dennis. 'I know.' He had recalled one of the Major's pet sayings: 'Don't advertise what you are going to do. Just do it.'

Prowling on looking for Exocets to blow up, Barky began to feel the warm feeling evaporating. Time was running out. The shouts lifting from unseen men, yelling in Spanish, sounded heavier. The words battered out with authority. In Barky's book that meant someone was getting his finger out and knocking some sense back into his men.

This confusion had to end soon. Huey and Sniper up on the cliff top could only keep up the charade for so long and then they'd have to pack up and leave. If they hadn't drawn the majority of the Argies up there by then, the lads on the beach would not have things their own way. Where, murmured Barky to himself fuming, where in hell are these flaming Exocets?

A few moments later, the bedlam still unended, he reached a small area of beach which seemed to be cleared of obstruction. A dead Argentinian soldier lay on the ground. He'd been shot through the back, and he was not a pretty sight.

'Shot by his own pals,' said Deadly in a disgusted tone of voice.

'Yeah. Poor devil. Sooner him than us.'

Then the world seemed to erupt in a scarlet billow of flame and a devastating explosion. Deadly and Roller smashed backwards. Barky felt the blast rip at his head and shoulders. He staggered, tripped and fell. Gritty sand wedged into his mouth, clogging his teeth, tasting vile on his tongue. His head rang. He was lying with his face rammed into the ground, all the bells in Saint Paul's ringing in his skull and his body feeling as though a wrestler had slammed him down repeatedly

He tried to claw up. His eyes were full of tears. In a ghastly distortion of reality he saw Deadly and Roller sprawled out. Both men moved. Their arms and legs twitched. Barky dragged in a lungful of air. It hurt.

'Deadly,' he managed to croak out. 'Roller!'

Roller sat up. He spat sand. Deadly put his right hand to his left shoulder. His face twisted.

'Buggers got me.'

'Let's see.'

Barky, using willpower he didn't even know he possessed, shoved himself up onto his knees. He crawled rather than walked across to Deadly, walking for the moment quite beyond him.

'In the shoulder.' Deadly removed his spread fingers cautiously. The grenade fragments had made a nasty mess. Already thick black blood glistened evilly within the rip in the camouflage material.

'Most of the force was spent,' said Roller. 'We were too far away from the grenade.' His face looked mean. 'I'd like to –'

'Save it. Give me a hand with Deadly.'

'Yeah. Right.'

'And,' said Barky, 'don't shout. We're all half deaf by now, I shouldn't wonder.'

Whoever had tossed the grenade had not followed up the attack. Shrimp, following along outside the danger area, checked out possible sites. If an Argie was hiding in the shadows between stores, he'd be damned difficult to pick out. Shrimp searched carefully, his face almost like that of a gargoyle in the erratic illumination.

'Can't see anybody. He's scarpered.'

'All the same,' said Barky.

'Yeah.' Shrimp moved forward at the ready, taking up a position to cover his comrades.

With fastidious care, Barky started work on Deadly's shoulder. The grenade fragment had sliced through the anorak and vest, ripping into Deadly's flesh. Just how deep the wound was Barky didn't know. He fished out his first aid medic pack.

'Blighters,' spat Deadly. Then he added in a surly voice, 'Bastard Argie had guts, though.'

'Sure. Now wrap up while I patch you up.'

'There's no one about here, now,' said Shrimp.

Barky wondered, surmising in a way he didn't altogether like, if perhaps Strike Force was getting too big for its boots. Maybe they'd taken this whole thing too casually. Maybe they were getting stale.

Then he roused himself. No. No, he wouldn't have that. The Major would know. Trouble was, the Old Man had copped a packet over on the Argentinian mainland and was out of it on SS *Uganda*. Barky, along with Tom Burnaby, had felt that Strike Force might collapse without the Major there to counsel and guide – and to drive them on relentlessly. He'd fought against that feeling. He'd made up his mind that Strike Force, and Number Three Wing for which he was responsible, would soldier on. They wouldn't cave in now. No, sir!

Roller said, 'I'm all right, Barky. Shrimp and me'll recce ahead.'

'Check. And find those confounded Exocets.'

All the time this had been going on, Barky had been working on Deadly's shoulder. Thankfully, he saw the wound was nowhere as serious as he had first thought. The heavy DPM cloth and the clothing beneath had been sufficient to take most of the impact from the grenade fragment. It had gouged a rip out of Deadly's flesh, given him some pain, and made him even more annoyed than he had been.

'Keep your hand stuffed inside,' cautioned Barky. 'Keep the weight off your shoulder.'

'Yeah,' snarled Deadly. 'Me and Napoleon.'

The big fifty calibre Browning blasting from a cave entrance further along continued to spread its fire at random across the beach.

Barky glared about. Deadly stood up, swayed once, and was himself.

'Let's get after them, Barky. "Vengeance is mine, sayeth the Lord". This is so. But I'm going to help out personally.'

They started off along the beach again, tracking Roller and Shrimp.

Crouched at the foot of the cliff, SS and Dingle watched the long tongue of flame from the heavy machine gun. Bullets were flying everywhere. They sprayed indiscriminately, occasionally the whining strike of a ricochet cutting through the uproar.

'Great Wally,' observed SS.

'Scared down to his socks,' confirmed Dingle.

Neither man took his attention from what was going on out on the beach, their gazes constantly roving over the sandy grit, the piles of stores, the fuzzy patches of illumination where the Argies had left a working light burning.

They heard Punch's raspy voice from over their heads.

'Comin' down.'

They didn't turn or tilt their heads up to look at Punch climbing down the ladder. They'd seen that before.

For what could have been no longer than three heart beats the staccato of the sub-machine gun, blending with the clatter of the Browning fifty calibre, fooled them.

Both men spotted the twinkle of flame from the SMG together. The indistinct form of the Argie shooting up at the cliff blended with a stack of boxes, the last few tumbled haphazardly onto the ground, left as they'd fallen when the soldiers carrying them had run off.

With a ferocious roar and a thumping crash Punch dropped free from the ladder.

SS and Dingle fired together.

Their rounds slammed into the vague figure and knocked it back, sprawling, into the shadows. The SMG fire spewed upwards, scything empty air, and stopped.

Jack 'The Joker' Dexter hung onto the ladder. He gripped the rungs with both hands. He could feel this body hanging. He swallowed convulsively. He couldn't move.

'Come on down here, you scented narner!'

'Yeah. Yeah. Coming. Yeah, right.'

Somehow Dexter returned to reality. He concentrated on holding onto the rungs of the ladder. One rung at a time. Hand under hand, boot below boot, get himself safely down to the ground.

The sight of those evil little pocks stuttering across the face of the cliff towards him remained vividly in his mind. He thrust the memory away. That was over. The Argie had not shot him. His boot hit the ground, he released the death clutch and stepped away from the ladder.

Punch, enormous, confident, rallying them on, bellowed, 'Next cave! Tally ho!'

'Tally ho?' said Dexter. 'Who's the scented narner now, then?'

There was no need for Punch to point out how right he had been to detail SS and Dingle in the way he had. If they'd been off blowing up Exocets on their own account, Dexter certainly and probably Punch, too, would be lying sprawled out riddled with sub-machine gun bullets.

Being the sort of fellow who'd kick your teeth in during a fight and then stand you up and brush off your clothes for you, Punch said: 'Right. SS, Dingle, you two can have the next hole.'

Shortly after the two oppos had vanished into the cave, with Punch and Dexter on watch below, Dingle stuck his head out. He looked disgusted.

'Nothing but grub up here.'

'Well, get your arse out of it. We'll hit the next one. Jump!'

The next cave opening did not yield Exocets mounted on ground launchers. Instead, a totally enraged Punch kicked a carton containing toilet rolls. They spewed out and rolled merrily about the dusty cave.

'Really setting up shop, here, the Argies,' said Dexter.

'Yeah. And they're gonna need these, too!'

At the next cave opening Dingle stuck his head out and yelled triumphantly.

'Bingo!'

'All right, all right. Castrate the bleeding things.'

Working speedily, SS and Dingle packed plastic where it would do the most good and set the timers. If the law of averages was maintained, then here were two

British warships saved from being sunk.

The Browning fifty calibre finally stopped shooting.

'Run out of ammo, the silly sod,' said SS.

Looking down from the cave mouth and ready to drop down the ladder, Dingle rapped out, 'Here comes Barky.'

Moving up swiftly, Barky saw Dingle give a brief wave and then start down the ladder. Moments later he saw Punch and the Joker. Then SS appeared and slid down the ladder. They crouched down together, watchful, ready for the next phase in the operation.

'Rommel?' said Punch.

'Rommel,' said Barky. 'Yeah. Those boats should've gone up by now.'

At that moment, as though Rommel had heard them, massive explosions broke from the shoreline.

The Argentinian Special Forces troops they'd spotted climbing up the rocks would be the signal for Huey and Sniper to break off their display and retire gracefully from the scene. They'd rendezvous at the first or second rally points. That meant the Special Forces people who'd just clambered up the headland would have to start going down again to investigate the explosions created by Rommel at the shoreline.

Punch said: 'We ought to mallet a few as they come down.'

Barky just said: 'Exocets.'

'Yeah. Well.'

Bunce and Chunky appeared with fresh supplies of plastic. Punch's patrol kitted up with the feeling that unless they moved very fast and were extremely lucky they might not get to use the explosive that night.

'We'll split the rest of the cave openings,' said Barky. 'Time's running out.'

They set off like eager beavers, breaking into their respective teams to tackle the remaining caves. Just how many missiles had been brought ashore they could only guess. From the quantity of general stores being shifted up from the beach, Barky estimated from his limited experience that a kit of four, or even six missiles, might be the total. The teams checked each cave in turn.

A few hostiles were discovered. These were mainly technicians who, very sensibly, had taken cover. As long as they did not interfere with the Strike Force's work, they were untouched.

During the rapid inspection of one of the smaller caves, choked with ammunition boxes, Barky ran across a crate of white phosphorus grenades. They were disgusting things. If Deadly had been in the way of one of those he wouldn't be keeping watch by the ladders and cursing a wounded shoulder. If he hadn't already died from horrific burns, Barky knew with revulsion that the kindest thing would have been to shoot him.

He set the marzipan-like charges, timed them and scuttled back down the ladder.

Because of the white phosphorus grenades, now due to be blown sky-high, Barky committed the solecism of asking Deadly how he felt.

'The Good Lord saw fit to extend the mantle of his protection over me, Barky. I ain't gonna fall down just yet.'

Bunch reported that he'd turned up a 'Bleeding Exocet' and had primed it ready for the off. Barky checked his watch.

'Five of 'em,' he said.

'Couple more caves to go yet,' pointed out Deadly.

'Yeah. Roller, you and Shrimp keep your obbo on

those Special Forces blighters. Minute they show up, yell.'

'Check.'

Roller and Shrimp departed at speed. Again Barky consulted his watch. 'Five minutes. That's all. After that, we scarper.'

Punch and Dexter copped the last hole in the cliff. They shinned up the ladder with SS and Dingle keeping watch. This cave mouth held a surprise. None of the others had been covered from the outside; this one had a blanket draped like a curtain from the roof to the floor. Cautiously Punch put an eye to a fold at the bottom and squinted up.

At his back Dexter poised with a grenade in his fist.

The light made little swimming black spots before Punch's eyes. He blinked and adjusted his sight quickly. He swore.

The place had been furnished with a carpet, chairs and a table. A curtain draped from poles in the walls half-concealed a bed. The bed was a real one of heavily-carved mahogany. These things, and the other odd bits and pieces of furnishing endeavouring to make the place more comfortable were not what caused Punch's exclamation.

In a soft whisper heard only for about three feet, he said: 'Tell Barky. There are three women up here, all scared out of their wits, half-naked, and what the hell do we do about them?'

CHAPTER TEN

In normal circumstances no one in Strike Force would have been at a loss for an answer to that question.

Now, with some people running about shooting off sub-machine guns and throwing grenades, and others blowing things up, amid fire, noise and general pandemonium, Barky did the only thing he could.

'Hoick 'em out of it,' he called back up to Dexter. 'We can't leave the poor things there. This whole cliff is due to blow.'

'Check.'

'One under each arm for me,' said Punch when Dexter relayed Barky's message.

'Yeah.' Dexter slung his Enfield IW. 'And what're you going to use to hold onto the ladder?' But, very sharply, he added, 'No, don't tell me.'

Punch ripped the curtain aside. The three women reacted more or less as he'd expected they would, screaming and wailing, which mightily upset him, for he was a sensitive fellow when it came to the finer feelings of ladies. Whether or not these three women would be classified as ladies was irrelevant now. They were females in distress and that was quite enough to make all Punch's finer feelings flower.

'Quieten down, ladies,' he rapped out, and then, in a more placating tone, 'Silencio.'

They went on yelling as though Punch was the very devil himself, horns, tails, the lot. Dexter tried a spot of his execrable Spanish. The ladies were neither old nor young, but of a certain age, as the saying had it. They were dark of hair, swarthy of face, and fiery of eye. And they kicked up one hell of a racket.

They clutched the ivory lace of their nightdresses, or peignoirs, or negligées – it was unclear to the two oppos quite what the garments the ladies wore were.

'We'll have to grab 'em, Joker.'

'Seems like it.'

The pecking order seemed to be first the lady with the arrogant nose and longest hair, second the one with the large breasts slopping about and a face streaked with tears and lastly the youngest, who had a far more slender waist than the others.

Dexter made a dive for her. She screamed and lashed out with her small yet knobbly fist. Dexter caught her arm, gave her his most brilliant smile, and apologising, 'Pardon me, senorita,' twisted her around and slung her over his shoulder. Her legs kicked splendidly.

'Tally ho!' yelped Punch and dived in.

He aimed for number two, handling her as gently as he could and trying not to let her ample bosom interfere with his concentration and grip. He turned to follow Dexter and lady number one simply threw herself at him.

In a collapsing heap they sprawled onto the carpet. A hard-edged chunk of the rock floor gouged into Punch's ear, and he ripped out an outraged curse.

Flailing around in an effort to sit up, he got a mouthful of very soft, very sloppy breast. He used language that

Dexter, turning to watch in fascination, trusted the ladies would not understand. He was under no illusion that had the language Punch was spitting out so freely been Spanish they would not have been entirely familiar with every nuance.

Dexter could not stop himself from laughing. 'Enjoying yourself, Punch?'

'I'll – glumph, glumph – I'll have you for this, Joker!'

Punch spat out negligée, got a fresh grip and pushed lady number one away so that she fell over onto her bottom shrieking her head off, then roared up to follow Dexter from the cave.

The ladies had sense enough not to struggle over much as they were carried down the ladder. Reaching the ground, Punch fairly flung his girl at Barky.

'Here, Barky, hold onto her, for Pete's sake.'

Dexter placed his girl down gently on the ground, still holding her around the waist and staring into her tear-streaked face. He gave her that smile of his. She swallowed down and opened her mouth to let rip a gargantuan shriek. Dexter could see the flakes of lipstick, the saliva, and the little hairs of her moustache. He shook his head and placed a hand over her mouth, still smiling.

She tried to bite him. That was perfectly normal, and he didn't mind, for she entirely failed to hurt him.

Punch swivelled around, snarling.

'All right, Roller! There's another one of 'em up there. You can go and get her.' Then he was cruel. 'She'll melt in your arms, Romeo.'

Roller looked hurt. They'd called him Romeo when he'd had trouble with a girl trying to do a spot of spying. But he recognised that Punch was incensed, so instead of snapping back he went up the ladder to find out what kind of lady they'd left him to rescue.

Barky had visions of the whole operation slipping away. Here they were, having placed charges on five Exocets, with the whole cliff ready to avalanche on top of them, playing tomfool Sir Galahads and rescuing senõritas in distress. It didn't bear thinking about.

Quite clearly he had to remove these women to a place of safety. He regarded that as his responsibility. He saw with relief that they were wearing slippers. Probably, despite its carpeting, the floor of the cave was hard on their tender little feet. Well, if they couldn't march they'd be carried. Time was now cutting very fine. He checked his watch again and frowned, and turning to look up saw Roller clambering down the ladder as though he carried a sack of potatoes wrapped in a parachute.

'All out,' he said.

A certain amount of jocular repartée and jostling for positions followed. Punch, Dexter and Roller wanted nothing to do with the ladies. Some of the other lads were quite eager to assist the girls. The three members of Strike Force who had already had contact with the senõritas let them get on with it.

Because of Deadly's shoulder Barky vetoed the idea that Deadly Dennis should carry one of the ladies. So Deadly intoned solemnly, and no doubt with frustrated malice, ' "Beware the sins of Babylon, my sons, for they are scarlet and profane before the Lord." '

'Hard luck, Deadly,' carolled Bunce, his powerful hands firmly dug into the buttocks of the lady over his shoulder.

'Grrr,' snarled Deadly.

Barky smiled at the men's banter. The uproar out on

the beach went on, Rommel's handiwork blazing to the dark sky and obscuring the stars in banners and coils of smoke. Now he had to extricate Number Three Wing safely.

The outlying patrols would be pulling back now. Barky, with this group, was three or four minutes behind schedule. Time to saddle up and get a gallop on.

On the return trip they saw only two bundles of Argies. In both instances a brief burst of fire scattered the hostiles and opened a clear way.

The frame of mind of Strike Force now was such that they were squabbling over who should carry the ladies. They'd done the job. In only moments now, judging by the sweep of the second hands of their watches, the Exocets should be blown to kingdom come. A swift, safe trip through the wire, avoid the mines, and they'd be away and dry.

Intense physical effort, the absolute concentration on what had to be done, the care and caution needed to ensure no one was hurt and no one fouled up – all these pressures would take their toll. That would come later. No time now to dream about disasters or triumphs, no time to sweat, no time to do anything but leg it back through the wire and the mines.

Just as they reached the wire, the crash of explosions along the nearer shoreline indicated where Rommel had been adding to his workload. Barky hauled up and caught Punch's arm.

'We can't just take off and leave the women here, Punch. They'll go screaming back to find their friends, the charges will blow, and –'

'And the whole flaming cliff will fall on their heads.'

'Precisely.'

'I'm telling you, Barky, I ain't staying.'

Bunce shoved up, big and burly, his Armalite slung. Since that first little trip with a lady over his shoulder he considered he hadn't had his fair share. 'I'll hang on, Barky.'

'Righto, my son. Not too long, mind.'

'I'll stay, too,' said SS.

Dingle gave his oppo a good hard look, but said nothing.

'The moment the plastic does its duty, clear out. We'll be on the other side to give covering fire if necessary.'

With that settled they started through the wire. The bang, when it finally came, sounded like Mount Everest falling.

Barky swivelled to look back. He'd seen pictures of open-cast mining in foreign countries where they laid a series of charges in bore holes down a cliff edge and then blew them in succession. The complete face of the hill was ripped off. It was like taking a slice of bread off a loaf. The uproar went on and on, prodigious, immense, overpowering. Blackness shot through with vivid tongues of orange and yellow flames spurted over everything. If those poor fool women had been left to their own devices, chances were they'd have been under that lot.

There was no possible chance, in Barky's book, that the Exocets had survived. All that remained would be unrecognisable bits of twisted metal. And a good job too.

Negotiating the mine panel through the gap made earlier demanded concentration and care. They crawled with a careful devotion to self-preservation.

Out past the last marker, Barky let out a whoosh of pent-up breath. He just didn't *like* mines.

'If that idiot SS messes about,' grumbled Dingle.

No need for Barky to give orders to spread out and be ready to give covering fire. The patrols shook out, weapons at the ready. Rommel and his party came in and everyone settled down for what they all hoped would be a short wait. The air choked with dust and debris. The infernal noise of the chain of explosions echoed in their heads.

Dexter experienced no surprise whatsoever as his oppo started to jabber.

'What a bang!' said Punch. 'Luvverly!'

No one replied.

'That'll show 'em,' went on Punch. 'They can't mess about with us and get away with it.'

Rommel snapped, 'Shut up, Punch.'

Swiftly, Dexter intervened, 'Any sign of SS and Bunce?'

'Nah.'

Just as Barky was seriously beginning to think he'd have to send someone back, or go himself, to rake out the two missing men, a dark lump appeared heaving along the cleared path.

SS wormed through and swivelled to look back.

'Nice one,' he said, then added, 'No sign of hostiles, Barky. Bunce should be on my heels.'

'The women?'

'Good job we held onto 'em. They'd have gone running into that lot like headless chickens. They'll be gone now, though, gone to tell their boyfriends about us.'

'Yeah.'

'Take some time before they get their wits together,' Deadly judged.

'Reckon.'

Rommel, in his typical ineffable way said: 'There were Argie Special Forces blokes around.'

'Surely.'

'Well, then.'

'Leave it out, Rommel!'

Punch cut in, 'Looks like Bunce now.'

They all watched as the indistinct dark figure inched nearer. It seemed to Barky a trifle off the centre line of the cleared path.

He opened his mouth. He was going to risk a low-pitched hail to call out: 'Watch it, Bunce. Get to the centre, your right.'

Before he could speak a flash of light followed by a bang erupted from the minefield.

'Oh, no!' someone yelled.

Barky was up and surging forward. Dexter was with him. They reached Bunce.

He lay on his side, his body contorted, one hand reaching down past his knee. Barky could not see any foot attached to the lower leg. He didn't say anything. He felt so much anger and remorse, so much gut-spewing violence he was trembling all over.

Dexter got a hand and arm under Bunce's shoulders.

Bunce managed to gabble out, 'All right. I'm all right.'

'Sure, Bunce. Relax, lie easy. We'll get you out of this.'

Between them, Barky and Dexter hauled and carried Bunce through the rest of the mine panel. Greasy darkness smeared from the amputated leg.

Deadly had a first aid dressing ready. He said nothing. Bunce was in shock. They dressed the stump. They hoisted him up, and Punch took the burden, no one offering to contradict him. They started out. They could feel the savageness of their anger boiling and seething inside them, but they could do nothing about it right now.

Bunce, one of Special Strike Force, blown up on a mine, his foot sheared off.

That was right out of order.

It was just another part of the price they were paying down in the South Atlantic.

CHAPTER ELEVEN

They found themselves a hide in which to go invisible for the day and made Bunce as comfortable as possible.

All Corporal Dan Taylor could think of was his Armalite.

'Dropped it,' he kept mumbling in his half-conscious state, the drugs working on his tough body, trying to send him drifting off to dreamland. 'Dropped it in the mire.'

Everybody in Strike Force knew of the horror entertained by Bunce regarding his MI6. He, like them all, knew of the horrendous disasters suffered by the Americans in Vietnam when the soldiers believed publicity telling them that the new Armalite rifles did not need to be cleaned. With the change in propellent powder from the factory the rifles had fouled and, as a natural consequence, had jammed.

Bunce was fanatical about keeping his MI6 scrupulously clean. He was so often joshed about it that it had become a running joke in the Force. And now, this.

Just before, thankfully, he went right under, he said, 'Y'know, Romeo, you was bloody lucky being the messenger wallah that day. I never got a chance at Françine. She was ... She was ...'

'He's just rambling,' said Dexter, sharply. 'The spaced-out narner. Poor old Bunce. That's a Blighty one and no mistake.'

Roller was not impressed by Dexter's attempt at pacification. Yes, of course poor old Bunce had copped one and of course he hadn't had a chance at Françine. Roller had. She'd been working for a freelance spy called Vadim, using a wimp called Gervase, and between them and the threat of Françine's husband Arnaud, they'd tried to rig Roller with photographs. Roller was proud of those that showed him and Françine in bed and in action. The pictures of him in compromising homosexual activity with Gervase, taken whilst Roller had been drugged and in no condition to know what was happening to him, were entirely different. Still, the Major and Strike Force had sorted that lot out. Vadim had for a time been let loose on a long rein, fed false information about a mythical organisation dubbed Lightning Reaction Squadron.

Then came the day when more positive action had to be taken. MI5 and Special Branch, brought in because the Major insisted that his command must operate within the Law, reported their conviction that Vadim's usefulness had almost expired.

He worked on his own account and he had a small apparat. He found things out and sold them to the highest bidder. His interest in SSF had been aroused through his contact with a poor devil of a captain in Whitehall who'd either been pushed or had jumped from a hotel window. If Vadim could uncover the facts of Special Strike Force there would be plenty of eager buyers in the Intelligence departments around the world.

Major Dan Granville had pointed out, more than once,

that Strike Force was a *secret* organisation.

With those eerily-pale slatey eyes bright under the foreshortened brim of his cap, his reddish moustache bristling, he'd announced, 'Friend Vadim is due for the chop.'

They were all gathered around in the mangy little hut they called HQ. The sun was shining beautifully, the flowers were in full bloom and the air was sweet and invigorating.

'Let me –' began Roller.

'No, Romeo. You're out of this one.'

'Major!'

'Leave it out, Roller,' said Barky. 'The Major's right, as usual. When this one goes down you'll be –'

'I'll be peeling the spuds, I suppose!'

'If you so desire.'

'There is no argument.' The Major banged his swagger stick down on the plain wooden table. Not a single man of Strike Force jumped. 'Romeo, you'll be on the Gunjepoo end of the proceedings.'

Part-mollified, Roller said, 'Very good, Major.'

Vadim had, according to Smyjo, tried to be too clever. He had not so much played both ends against the middle as played both ends and the middle at the same time. The intelligence officer had liaised with the responsible authorities and the picture was that Vadim was selling the false information about LRS to various high-level powers. He was also finalising arrangements to sell information to Gunjepoo of Nariscia, and as it looked possible that arrangements would have to be made about that country steps had to be taken immediately.

'But if they're all evil-minded,' Andy wanted to know, 'do we take sides?'

The Major brushed up one side of his moustache. 'Our primary objective is the protection of British interests and British citizens. We leave all political decisions to those elected to take them. Is that clear?'

'Yes, Major,' came the chorus.

'Right, then. Smyjo is writing an op paper. Final positions will depend on a number of factors which I won't go into now.'

He liked to tantalise his men, did Major Dan Granville. Keep 'em on their toes, he'd say, with a piercing stare from his hard eyes.

'Can't take you all, and there are other pots boiling to be taken care of. Those involved will be informed.'

Looking at Bunce, lying unconscious in the hide, his face haggard and lax, Barky could not help contrasting his present appearance with the time they'd been involved in the Gunjepoo affair. War was a stinking business and no place for sane grown-up men.

This mood would pass. He'd fight off this fit of the black-dog, just as he always did. Just that ... Well, better to collect himself and get on with the job in hand.

They called HQ and reported success and failure to Noggy. Noggy expressed himself of the opinion that he supposed five Exocets were worth one foot, but it was not the sort of bargain he'd like to make a habit of.

The salient fact about Strike Force was that essentially Strike Force always fought for Strike Force. When all the blood, sweat and tears, all the sacrifices had gone, what remained was Strike Force looking out for Strike Force.

Noggy relayed the information that the boats would be sailing in that night. Number Three Wing was recalled.

'Just get the operating theatre ready for Bunce.'

Then, Barky added viciously, 'Bloody mines.'

'Yeah. Bloody mines.'

The day dragged by with a careful watch, regular brew-ups, and the lads thinking of home, of what remained to be done here, of women and drinks, of sport and music, and of Bunce's foot.

Inevitably, in these circumstances, Barky broke a home-made rule and thought of Linda. He'd sworn he wouldn't. But, of course, he did.

She was one of the hang-gliding crowd. She possessed a mastery of the air that inspired Barky. He hadn't taken much notice of her at first, up there on the break of the Downs behind Shoreham. Up there the updrafts and thermals offered splendid opportunities for soaring flight that knocked a fellow over with the wonder of freedom and lightness and a wide-winged spurning of the ground beneath. Also, there was a damned lot of skill and cunning needed to shift the body around and take all the opportunities the air offered.

She turned out to be an artist down from Art College wasting her time in an advertising agency and lucky to get the job.

One of the fellows, a beefy, beer-gutted idiot called Giles, kept on in a stupid way about her painting his portrait. With a revoltingly sly giggle he offered to pose, as he phrased it, *au naturel*. She cut him up and diced him but he still wouldn't take no for an answer. In the end Barky was called for his flight. By the time he returned Linda was sitting alone looking a trifle red about the ears. There was no sign of Giles or his car.

So Barky offered her a lift, the offer was accepted, and they drove back together. That was the start of it.

The trouble with being in SSF was that they couldn't

be honest about what they did. To family and those who knew them before, the fact that they were in the Army was patent. Then they were 'off on manoeuvres, or tied down to a nice cushy office job.' To those who didn't know them they could be anything. Roller was an insurance man. Barky, unable to be in advertising, suggested he was a sales rep. Linda did not enquire further. Unhappy in her own meaningless job, she turned to the doings of the day to fill her mind.

That mind was active and alert. She liked new things and anything that came along that intrigued her she lapped up like a kitten does cream. Also, she was well-educated in those aspects of civilization Barky knew to be important and which had generally escaped him. Like modern art and modern classical music, although he demurred at the fatuity of such a name for such –

'Don't you dare call it rubbish, Miles!'

'Well it takes years and years to develop anything you can call classical.'

'I know. That isn't the point.'

'No good your trying to educate me. Eight notes in an octave are good enough for me, and a face with only two eyes, one each side, will do to be going on with.'

'Philistine.'

For obvious reasons Barky couldn't take her home, so they sat and drank tea in the shambles of a flat she shared with three other girls. They saw each other as often as Barky could wangle leave or the odd day off. Their relationship blossomed. Then, one early evening of mellow sunshine and that odd hush that falls over London between bouts of hectic activity, she offered to paint his portrait.

The other three girls were all out on dates.

He stared at her. Linda was not what he would call beautiful, but she had freshness and vitality. Her eyes were wide spaced, brown, charming. Her nose was the right shape and size and her mouth eminently kissable. She was not in the same league as that girl Tom Burnaby was interested in – if the girl Barky had seen up on stage shedding her clothes was the right one. Beauty like that could be dangerous, poisonous. Linda was cuddly, nice.

'All right.' Then he went on to say what had been in his mind for some time, and had remained there unspoken because he knew she'd cut him down to size if he dared.

'All right. And I'll paint you.'

She laughed. Her teeth were white and even, with only a chip out of the top corner of her left front tooth.

'I know you, Miles Barker! You'll offer to paint me, not a picture of me. Get off!'

'Well, it was worth a laugh.'

She set up her easel and equipment with a casual expertise that impressed him. He knew all the paraphernalia of painting did not come cheaply. He'd have to buy the flaming thing off her, if she'd let him.

'Just your face,' she said. 'For now.'

The portrait consumed three whole leaves. He managed to kiss her a few times, and that was splendid; nothing else transpired and he was oddly perfectly willing to let the relationship roll along at her pace.

Deadly spoke up, 'Parcel of Argies heading this way.'

Barky roused himself. 'Check with the Joker. See if that creep Caldeiro's with 'em.'

Dexter came on to the air: 'Can't see the turdhead. But then, he'd detail his patrols out. He wouldn't turn up until they report they've found us.'

'Yeah,' came Punch's aggressive tones. 'If it wasn't for Bunce it'd be a good idea to let them spot us and send for that turdheaded creep. Then –'

'Negative on that one, Punch, for now. Good idea, though.'

'Yeah.'

The Argentinians passed. They wore odd flat berets that stuck out like plates, or funny little woollen caps. They looked useful, as though they knew what they were doing.

'If they're the lot who go around making people disappear,' said Deadly in Barky's ear, 'then may the wrath of the Lord descend upon them from a great height.'

Itch though he might to have a go at the hostiles, Barky had to contain the instinct to attack. They had done a good job here, had put out of action five Exocets and had created some degree of apprehension in the Argies infesting these parts.

His first concern now must be to see to Bunce. No one was going to be happy trying to casevac him if Barky stayed on and the operation took place in the middle of a firefight.

Intermittent bursts of profane description of just what Punch would like to do to the turdheads who'd roughed up his oppo created ripples of amusement. The business was serious, deadly serious where people could be killed – or have a foot blown off – but the British soldier's often macabre sense of humour would never be denied.

The sun sank and the breeze died. Well before midnight in response to wireless signals and the blue light, the launch hove up and evacuated Special Strike Force, Number Three Wing, bearing its casualty from that part of West Falkland.

CHAPTER TWELVE

Funny how the proceedings of briefing sessions varied. Sometimes, in Barky's experience, they ran like clockwork. At others there seemed no end to foul ups, arguments and general misunderstandings.

The whole of Special Strike Force had flown across to Canada, all masquerading under false identities. Over there they could run about like crazy and shoot off masses of live ammo with the nearest civilians hundreds of miles away.

Rommel scrounged time to go and visit the nearest tank unit and came back in a chastened mood. He commented, only half mockingly, 'I'm still not entirely used to going about without a nice thick slab of armour between me and the nasties.'

'You get caught in one of those perambulating monstrosities,' Pugsy told him, 'when the Orange folk start up their Saggers and RPGs and whatnots, and you're in your own coffin.'

'My old 120 would blow 'em away before they even knew I was around.'

'You hope.'

After that brisk little loosening of the muscles and arteries, Strike Force was sent on leave by the Major with the promise that when they rejoined they'd be in for the Gunjepoo op. That suited the lads.

So when Barky reported to the Intelligence Colonel, he was thinking of the briefing the Major had given that time. Number Three Wing had rested up for a space, washed, eaten, drunk and generally brought themselves back to a condition in which they were ready for their next assignment.

This Colonel of Intelligence was the same Colonel who had given Barky his instructions to take a map ashore on the beaches near Port Stanley in order to deceive the Argentinians into believing that the Task Force intended to make a big attack there, knocking on the front door of the Falklands. Whether or not that ploy had succeeded, Barky, of course, had no way of knowing. What he did know was that the Argies had in the main stayed clustered about Stanley and had made no effort to oppose the landings at San Carlos.

Two Para had done a marvellous job at Goose Green, but had suffered casualties which upset everyone. They'd gone in with about four hundred and fifty men, and for the price of fifteen dead and thirty wounded had killed or captured over thirteen hundred Argentinians. Jubilation, at least in Strike Force, was muted. The maroon machine had lost good men.

The breakout from the bridgehead around San Carlos was on. The Marines were yomping eastwards and the Navy was happily blowing up targets pointed out to them. Barky, remembering his recent experiences with Naval Gunfire Support, just hoped the Royal Navy's gun wouldn't jam too often.

'Fifth Infantry Brigade is on the way out to reinforce,' the Colonel told Barky. 'Apart from all the support arms, they have 2nd Battalion Scots Guards, 1st Battalion Welsh Guards, and 1st Battalion 7th Duke of Edinburgh's Own Gurkha Rifles.'

'Gurkhas,' said Barky. 'They'll put the wind up the Argies.'

'I'm sure. East Falkland is now crawling with Special Forces. Your Number One Wing, with Two in support, is out there.'

Barky saw at once what was coming. 'You're not telling me there's no room for us?'

'Certainly there is no room, at the moment, with the forces already on the ground.'

'Well, hell's bells and buckets of blood! I'm not tamely sitting it out aboard ship.'

'You won't be, Lieutenant.'

Two pips were mighty small beer set against a crown and two pips. All the same, this Colonel of Intelligence had experience of the funny ways of Special Forces. He gave a frosty smile that twitched his cropped moustache and went on, 'We've had word from a wireless ham who's been contacted by elements of the Argentinian Army in East Falkland. They're disenchanted with what's going on. Now we've landed and are heading for Stanley, these Argies would like to talk.'

'Yes?'

'More specifically, they offer us a complete plan of the Argentinian minefields around Stanley. You can see how important that is.'

'Yes.'

Oh, sure. Oh, yes, bloody marvellously sure. Barky could see how important that information was. When the squaddies went in they'd know where to put their clumping great size nines and not have them blown off like Bunce's foot had been.

Bunce had been attended to and was mending but he'd never be able to run and jump like he had. Oh, he'd get around on a clever prosthetic foot, a chunk of wood or plastic. But he would never be the same old Bunce they knew.

'Mines,' said Barky. 'Mines.'

The Colonel gave him a sharp stare.

'You'll go in, rendezvous with the kelper and through him contact the defectors. If they have not already handed over the minefield charts, then they will hand them to you. It will be a quick in and out operation. Any questions?'

'No, sir,' said Barky in a voice that could have blown all the way from Antarctica. 'Just give me the details and I'll brief my Wing and we'll go and get the plans.'

'Very good, Lieutenant.' Then the Colonel added, 'And, good luck.'

Barky didn't trust himself to reply. *Bloody mines*!

He had to fight against the depression now threatening to drag him down. If, he'd told himself, if he knew what was nagging at him and causing the problem, then he could handle it. Well, he knew damn well what the problem was now. Bloody mines. And he still felt as depressed as hell.

Deadly took the opposite view.

'Great, right on. Once we get our German bands on those minefield plans we'll know where to step.' His voice thickened. 'Not like old Bunce.'

'Yeah. Yeah. Reckon.'

'What's this bloke's name, then?'

'Calls himself McCartney. Not his real name, callsign, I suppose. Understandable. If the Argies pick up his radio calls with his real name he's for the chop.'

'Him and his Argie defector buddies both.'

So, once again, Strike Force drew fresh kit, got themselves organised, and saddled up for a new operation.

As usual, the importance of what they were doing was not lost on them. The value of their work was clear. To prevent what happened to Bunce happening to a single soldier of the British forces was worth all the effort.

Yet, despite that knowledge, Barky realised he didn't feel the responses he regarded as appropriate. The old black dog was really at his throat now. How different this feeling was from the time when they'd crowded in for the Major's final briefing for the Gunjepoo op!

He'd just returned from the leave in which he'd managed to paint Linda. Just running the paint-loaded brush over her body made him realise the fascination of the artist's life.

She was absolutely scrumptious. By the time he'd finished they were both covered in paint. Using water-based pigments gave them the perfect opportunity for a shared bath. The water turned into the palette of a colour-crazed artist. And, as he reflected and tried not to, Linda really was a wonderful girl. He'd come back off that leave with the whole-hearted desire to stuff Gunjepoo's teeth down his throat at the very first opportunity and then grab another spot of furlough.

The Major intimated that a good job well done would indeed deserve more leave.

'The situation hasn't changed. Gunjepoo turns out to be the son, or maybe nephew, of the dictator himself. It is not really important. We don't need to know any of the political side of this op. He was abducted from some gaming hell-cum-brothel in the West End. His personal bodyguards were either shot, or they betrayed him. Anyway, there's no sign of any of 'em now.'

'Don't blame 'em,' said Guy.

'Yes, they do tend to do nasties to people over there. Right. The police have been keeping a low-key obbo on the place they're holed up in. It's pretty isolated. We've had models built so you can study all the angles and lay-out. The police, as you know, are none too keen to have their men charging in with firearms and getting themselves killed. Very sensibly they've asked for the professionals to go in. That's us – mainly because we are a completely unknown unit, unlike others who are very well-fitted for the task.'

Taking in the details of the briefing, Barky felt himself fascinated by the technical devices employed. The police had got onto the roof of the building unobserved and had lowered microphones down the chimneys to pinpoint the positions of terrorists, hostage and anybody else inside.

'The place is a country hotel, miles from anywhere. We think we have all the employees located inside. The manager and his wife, waiters, cook, cleaners, and so on. Their lives are at risk.'

'That's a bad business,' said Q.

'More so when our orders explicitly state that our top priority is to get Gunjepoo out alive. He may be the biggest bastard under the sun but, that's not our concern.'

'This year,' pointed out Smyjo, 'it's Gunjepoo's lot who are in power and the others who are the terrorists. Next year it could be the other way around.'

'And the whole operation must be kept under the tightest security wraps. We are not having tv cameras within a hundred miles.' The Old Man glared around at them. He went on, 'The police have kept it bottled up so far. The incident at the gaming club was passed off as gang warfare. No demands from the terrorists have been passed on. If their pals back home hear they could start Smyjo's turn around right away, and that wouldn't fit in at the moment.'

In his elegant laconic way, Guy said: 'We're all agog to hear who's going, Major.'

'The lists will be posted. The Vadim team have a job to do as well, you know.'

So, in an expectant frame of mind they split up to make their preparations. How different, Barky considered, how damnably different from here and now down in the South Atlantic, ready to go into East Falklands and see about a bloody minefield chart.

After proper medical attention, Deadly's shoulder gash was pronounced not fatal, and Deadly himself simply carried on. No one suggested he should stay behind when the lads went in. It was taken for granted that he would go with his comrades.

Jack the Joker Dexter was pleased that Deadly Dennis was fit. He still felt firmly convinced that Punch Fuller was not, but attempts to have Punch relegated to the HQ ship proved fruitless.

'I'm getting right cheesed off with you, Joker,' said Punch. He hunched his shoulders around, swinging his arms. 'I'm fighting fit. You trying to get me sent to the loony bin or sump'n?'

Useless for Dexter to babble that if he didn't care so much for Punch he wouldn't give a damn what he did. He could only try not to frown too hard and to say,

'Don't blame me if your fool head falls off just when we need it.'

'You won't get to playing footsie with my bonce, young Joker! Never you fear!'

So that was how, to his dissatisfaction, Dexter had to leave the position.

No one in the Wing cared much for an assignment that included mines. Bloody mines! Yet they were nowhere near as down in the mouth as Barky. They were convinced that what they were doing was worth doing, that it would save British lives, so they'd just damn well get on with it and hope it was over PDQ.

Although they were not as encumbered as usual, for this op was not expected to last long, they took a good supply of plastic explosive with them, just in case.

They roared along in their Rigid Raiders, spuming white water, the little craft kicking and bucking. When they got closer in they cut the engines and paddled the rest of the way in almost total silence. The muted splash of carefully handled paddles and the wash of the waves remained the only sounds to betray them.

They touched down well outside the heavily defended area around Port Stanley and prepared themselves for the hack across to the rendezvous. The weather had turned colder, as Rommel had predicted, and snow was well on the way. They settled down to the march and swung along, loaded down, eyes constantly alert and taking in everything of interest on the route.

They aimed to have reached their first marker point by dawn and hide out, finishing the hack the next night.

So here they were, marching along in a land swarming with hostiles. Who knew who was out there? The old, nasty feeling that an Argie with a sophisticated

American night sight was just lining up on you and about to press the trigger just had to be contained.

Just nip into the rendezvous, meet up with this fellow McCartney and his Argie pals, grab the minefield maps, and then hightail it out of there – that was the plan. During the day spent in their camouflaged hides they saw very little Argentinian ground activity. Some aerial movements took place and they saw Harriers screaming along and gave the Crabs a cheer.

Barky commented, 'Reckon the Argies are all hanging about Stanley, or manning the mountains over to the west.'

'They'll get their arses frozen off,' said Rommel with great satisfaction.

'May the Good Lord help 'em if the Gurkhas go in.'

'Chop, chop,' said SS. Dingle gave his oppo a look but said nothing.

Punch gave one of his subdued but nonetheless stentorian bellows. 'Them Argies should have stayed at home.'

'Oh,' said Dexter. 'I expect more than a few of them are thinking that themselves by now.'

'Saddle up,' said Barky. 'We'll be there in good time now.'

The plan called for them to reach the rendezvous, an isolated spot clear of the town itself, and hole up. The next night they could make the meet at midnight, as ordered, take the minefield charts and be well on their way out of it before they would need to take cover for the following day.

McCartney would get a clearance from his Argie defector pals to carry him through the curfew. No doubt he'd be in the middle of them, dressed as an Argie, and shielded by them from observation from unfriendly Argie patrols.

Barky intended to take no chances. He wasn't a newly born lamb to go to the butcher's shop. The Major would spit red hot rivets if anyone led a patrol of his beloved Strike Force blindly into an ambush.

Towards the Witching Hour, as Deadly put it, on the night appointed, he led off for the rendezvous. The temperature was well down, the night overcast, with a trifle of that blasted Falklands wind to ruffle them. The soggy ground gave silent going.

Punch in his aggressive way had stated that he wasn't going to be left out of the lot who had a dekko at McCartney and his Argie pals, which meant that Dexter went along too. SS and Dingle hacked along a trifle to the rear and flank. With Barky and Deadly Dennis up front and centre, they moved cautiously through the darkness.

Being Strike Force they arrived ahead of time, carried out a quick but thorough recce of the area, and then settled down to await the arrival of the contacts.

A few minutes after twelve dim figures showed ahead.

A torch flashed. A voice called softly: 'McCartney.'

'Starr,' called Barky, giving the pre-arranged countersign.

The figures neared. Barky counted automatically. There were ten of them.

'Seems friend McCartney has palled with quite a gang,' commented Punch.

'Shut the trap, Punch,' said Barky in an easy voice.

Punch shut up. With a bit of luck, Dexter considered, he was getting the message.

The ten approaching men fanned out to a semi-circle. The man in the centre, bulky in an Argentinian anorak, stepped out. Barky stepped up to face him. A torch flashed into Barky's face.

'You are most welcome. I am McCartney. You are?'

'You can call me Jones. Do you have the plans of the minefields?'

'Jones. Would that be Captain Jones?'

It didn't matter a damn. From sheer cussedness, Barky snapped out: 'Captain Jones, McCartney. We haven't got all night. Let me have –'

'Oh, yes, you will have it all right, Captain Jones.'

Dexter reared up. Enough light spilled back from the torch to cast a glow upon McCartney's face.

He saw the men still moving on to form a ring about them. Barky stiffened. He saw the light fall on McCartney's face and recognised it immediately.

'It's a trap!' he yelled. 'That's Captain Hector Caldeiro!'

CHAPTER THIRTEEN

'Very pleased to see you,' said Superintendent Bell. 'I'm totally opposed to sending my police officers into this kind of situation.'

'That's all right, Super,' said the Major in his best no-nonsense, matter-of-fact way. 'We'll take over now. But I'll expect full co-operation.'

'Of course.'

'You've left it rather late to call us in. If that latest deadline holds they'll start to shoot hostages at twelve hundred hours.'

'We've been through five deadlines in negotiation so far.'

'Just keep the updates coming in, Super, and we'll carry on.'

'Very good, Major.'

The country hotel taken over by the terrorists was a charming olde worlde place with a few outbuildings in mellow rose-red bricks, a number of intricately twisted chimneys and corresponding bay and oriel windows, and a complex roofing system that gave ample concealment for the police listening teams positioned there. Their microphones, gingerly lowered down the chimneys, picked up the locations of the people in the hotel. Their positions had been logged and a pattern established. Strike Force would not be going in blind.

The Major organised the patrols and teams. Everyone on the op had his assigned duty. This was, in a very real sense, a test for Major Dan Granville's Special Strike Force.

Deadly Dennis had expressed his opinion of Gunjepoo and the terrorists alike.

'Pernicious blots upon the fair face of the world,' he'd said, speaking with some feeling. 'So long as they're all right they don't give a damn for anything else.'

Trampas tipped his wideawake back and spoke with vehemence. 'Yeah. Like in the old days, when you could go around and kill peasants by the hundred, but you dared not kill a knight.'

'We have to get Gunjepoo out,' the Major reminded them, 'not for any concern over his unwholesome skin. There are British hostages in there, and it is essential this whole debacle is kept out of the media. Got it?'

'Got it.'

The police had created an access route from the back lane, using hedges and the greenhouses to afford complete cover up to the side of the rear yard. From there the way up to the roof could take a number of different sloping and treacherous angles. The chimneys had proved a slight problem, their twisted height creating the need for clever pole constructions and tripods in order to get the microphones inside.

The Major was told that this route remained secure. The twice-daily deliveries of food and drink, toiletries and cigarettes to the terrorists were made openly up the main drive. 'Then we've nothing to worry about. We could just wait,' the Major commented.

'Oh?' said Barky.

'Yes. If we don't kill 'em the cigarettes will.'

'Profound,' said Barky. 'Highly profound.'

'Wally,' chipped in Noggy. 'You mean deeply profound.'

All the same, no one in Strike Force missed the point of the Major's comment. They'd all seen, much to their disgust, young soldiers loitering about at railway stations or coach stations, smoking cigarettes, swearing, getting in the way, and generally acting like yobs.

It was almost always the very green young soldiers who behaved in this manner and, by the time they'd had a spot of training and discipline and understood a little more what being a real soldier entailed, most turned into professionals. If they cut up rough, reverting to adolescent behaviour in Germany, say, and upsetting the locals, some of that could be put down to frustration on the job.

It wasn't an easy task: to train and train your guts out learning how to kill people and then be told that under no circumstances will you be allowed even to get into a fight with anyone ...

Like any sensible commander, the Major was well aware of these and allied problems and was right on top of them.

'A trifle of pore-opening,' he said, beaming that chilly smile. 'Expand the lungs, get the old blood circulating. Get stuck in and for once you're off the leash.'

'Let slip,' commented Smyjo, 'the dogs of war.'

'And I want Gunjepoo alive.' The Major's flinty smile did not waver. 'Condition of the goods is of secondary importance beside the fact that they are still living and breathing.'

In order to look the part the terrorists had dressed in fancy black outfits. They wore high-necked sweaters, tightly-fitting black trousers and black Balaclavas with stocking masks positioned to be pulled over their faces when they contacted the authorities. No doubt they considered this sinister outfit would strike terror into the hearts of the hostages.

That it undoubtedly had done was not lost on the Major and the men of Strike Force. For their part they didn't give a damn what the opposition wore. If they were going to be malletted then they'd be killed no matter how fierce their rig.

The blokes from Strike Force went in simply wearing their normal combat gear, though they did paint up their tiger stripes, which made them seem their most menacing. In addition, the camouflage gave a measure of anonymity to each of them, and that was what the Major wanted: the fewer people who could recognise anyone in Strike Force the better.

Each man carried a sub-machine gun in addition to any specialist weaponry, for the shooting would be at extremely close quarters.

They had not yet been issued with scimitar wireless sets but were using standard pocket radios. They had what was considered an ample supply of stun grenades and when the crunch came they'd probably have to put on their respirators. A neat little ring of unpainted skin had been left to ensure good contact.

The Major commented that it was a pity that there was no inside wall they could work on. Had they been trying to deal with the terrorists in, say, a block of flats, they'd have had access to the inside walls. Then they'd cover the noise of their operations in some way, for instance with a battery of pneumatic drills, and dig out the bricks of the dividing wall. They'd pull them out by hand, one at a time, and make little more noise than a mouse behind the wainscoting. After that there would be only a thin sheet of plaster between them and the next door building. That wouldn't stop a hefty fellow from charging in with his SMG ready to fire, or a grenade to throw, alert to react to whatever he found inside.

Barky let drop a sarcastic snort.

'You know what Guy would say if he was here instead of off chasing after Vadim.'

'Yeah?'

'Yeah. He'd be thoroughly put out and disappointed if we had that opportunity. Guy thrives on being faced with apparently insurmountable obstacles he can find to put in our way.'

'Us and him, both,' pointed out the Major.

'Oh, yeah, surely.'

Weapons and equipment ready, the teams of Strike Force filed quietly along by the hedges and the glasshouses and reached the rear yard.

'Mind you,' said Pugsy, reflectively, 'if they stuffed this creep Gunjepoo and all the terrorists in the Glasshouse it'd do them all a power of good.'

'Leave it out,' said Spider. 'They'd fold inside half a day.'

The words were the usual mouth to ear. The Major half turned; Pugsy and Spider shut their traps and followed on silently.

Barky and his patrol started for the roof. He knew he was stupid to feel depressed over the fact that Punch and the Joker were not with him. They were off with Guy keeping tabs on Vadim and hoping to dovetail operations. As they cautiously crept onto the roof carrying climbing ropes, nappies, D-rings and Karabiners, Barky knew that Trampas and Jock would act just as effectively as any other pair of oppos in Special Strike Force.

As in any operation of this nature, timing was of paramount importance.

The police sergeant waiting for them beside a twisted chimney looked a trifle tense.

Barky cut out all the chatter; kept it strictly business. This was not just because he felt Strike Force should cut a certain figure in this murky world of chicanery. They were professionals, tight-mouthed, hard, here to do certain unpleasant things. There was no need for inessential chatter.

Location reports from the police listening teams were passed down to Major Dan Granville. He would collate these, with Smyjo doing the work, and decide the moment to go in.

Noggy and his patrol stationed themselves over on the other angle of roof beyond the central valley gutter. If Barky knew anything about old houses, that valley gutter and its ancient lead flashings would give constant trouble when it rained or snowed, the water would run down inside through the most minute of holes and channels. Then the ceilings would become soaked, and fall on the head of anyone unfortunate enough to be underneath.

'Keep well away from that valley gutter,' he told his patrol.

If one of them fell in before the rest – well, that was something Barky just wouldn't dwell on. The Major would spit red hot rivets, that was certain.

Keeping in constant contact, the various patrols and teams settled down.

For his part, The Old Man intended to wait until the police listening teams reported hostages and terrorists in exactly the right positions. From the patterns already established they shouldn't have long to wait. The hostages were mainly huddled in the dining room, where they had a little space in which to move. The terrorists tended to wander about the hotel, no doubt looking out of the windows to see what was happening. Terrorists in this situation were notoriously jumpy. As for Gunjepoo himself, the best intelligence suggested he was tied up in an upstairs bedroom.

Superintendent Bell and his liaison team placed their contact at the time instructed by the Major.

The guidelines for dealing with the terrorists were established. Each kind of terrorist had his own peculiarities, and the psychology of each type had to be determined as an immediate priority. Bell had this lot sorted to the extent that he felt uneasily convinced that they would not take the shilly-shallying of the authorities as genuine negotiation attempts for very much longer. If they started killing hostages, Bell, for one, would know a deep and distressing sense of failure.

His liaison team established contact in the normal way over the telephone and let the leader of the terrorists know that the mid-day supply of food, drink and cigarettes was coming in now.

After he had spent some time calming the excitable person on the other end of the line and reassuring them that everything was normal, he could feel sweat cold and clammy on his forehead in the bright sunshine.

'They'll open the front door,' he told the Major. 'The

inner one, wood with small glass panels, will be guarded by a terrorist with a tommy gun. The other door, all glass, opening onto the porch – you can see it from here – will be where the terrorist detailed to collect the supplies will wait.'

'Sniper,' said the Major in his metallic voice. 'You've got yourself your target.'

'Check,' said Sniper, and shifted his up-dated Lee-Enfield more comfortably over his shoulder.

'Obvious,' said the Major, 'but essential in these circumstances.'

'Time –' began Bell.

'Quite.'

Absolutely confident though he was in his shooting ability, Sniper felt a glow that the Major was so casually putting his life into his hands. Made a fellow feel good, that, made him feel a real part of the team.

Huey was there to back him up, and Ickey Frost and Bunce were ready to set off like the proverbial ferret down a rabbit hole.

Smyjon and Andy, without the need for last minute checks, took their leave of the Major and scuttled off quietly to their start positions. They would be acting as individuals, although going in shoulder to shoulder.

Sawbones, Captain Edward Parkes, RAMC, set up shop well back in the old lodge by the wrought iron gates that had once guarded the estate before it had been converted into an hotel. With him he had Dusty and Zeb.

Not all of Special Strike Force were involved in this Gunjepoo op, as the Major had promised. Tom Burnaby was detached on genuine work, and was totally unavailable, refusing to comment on the phone when the Major told him of the op. His absence had nothing whatsoever to do with his stripper. Anyway, as they all knew, Captain Tom Burnaby suffered from the illusion – delusion, more likely, as Barky crudely put it – that not a soul in Strike Force had an inkling of any stripper in his life.

He did say that it might be a pity he couldn't have got the supply of Heckler und Koch MP5A3 9 mm sub-machine guns into their hands in time. He'd happily fly out from West Germany with a supply if the Major gave the word.

'The old Hockler is a right useful tool, Major.'

'Quite so, young Burnaby. You get on with your task out there, and we'll make do with Uzis and Sterlings if we have to.' He spoke matter-of-factly. 'The Yard's C13 anti-terrorist squad are perfectly capable lads and we're here, so you do your duty there. Capisch?'

'Got it, major.'

Afterwards, the Old Man said to Smyjo, 'Tom sounded so brassed off I felt quite sorry for him.'

Smyjo passed a stiff forefinger over his upper lip. 'Tom's a very peculiar sort of bloke, major. Pity he's not here. He'd be useful.'

'True, true. You know my views. Everybody in Strike Force is useful, and we're all oppos.'

'Check, major.'

Often Smyjo had felt that if only some of the world's apparently insoluble problems were handed to the Major, they'd be sorted out in a trice. Arms limitation talks, for instance. If the hard-headed and pragmatic major got cracking on that, he'd have crisis management centres set up, all participants believing they were secure and happy and therefore not a threat to anyone else, and hot lines with full-scale direct picture and sound and translation facilities available twenty-four hours a day. Correction. If Major Dan Granville handled things it'd be twenty-five hours a day.

Smyjo and Andy took up their positions by the side of the glasshouses ready to go in. WO11 Andrew Stubbs could handle an Uzi just as well as he handled his SLR, even if in general circumstances he preferred a rifle to an SMG. He'd seen a bit of the world, in his time, had Andy, and had been in a number of hot spots as a very green youngster before returning home to join the Coldstreams.

With Noggy and his patrol on one roof, and Barky and his patrol on the other, the assault teams were all in position.

Backup was being provided in the first instance by Q, the Whizz Kid, and by Smartie and Brax.

All in all, decided the Major, the time was ripe and it was all systems go.

He spoke perfectly calmly into his microphone. 'Right. On my word you may begin the midday entertainment.'

He adjusted his white apron and hoisted his tray: '*Go*!'

CHAPTER FOURTEEN

'That's Captain Hector Caldeiro!'

The instant the words were out of his mouth Jack the Joker Dexter knew he had made a ghastly mistake.

The greasegun in Caldeiro's heavily-gloved hands twitched up.

'Yes, indeed, Englishman. I am Captain Hector Caldeiro. Stand perfectly still. I recognise you. Yes, indeed!'

Barky's Uzi snouted; he saw the muzzles of the weaponry pointing at him and thought he might get a burst off, take a few of the bastards out – but he knew he'd only take them down with him into Hell.

The ring of Argentinian Special Forces troops looked dark and menacing, their weapons now revealed and all aimed at the four Britons. A blood bath was only seconds away.

'Put down your weapons, Captain Jones.'

Through his teeth, Barky said: 'I could take you with me, Caldeiro.'

The handsome face within the shadow of the anorak hood highlighted by the glow of the torch showed amusement. Caldeiro was savouring his moment of triumph. Who could blame him?

'You have lost, captain. Bowled out for a duck, what? To resist any further would be unsportsmanlike, would it not?'

Barky clamped his lips. He wasn't going to get into an argument with an Argie about sport, for God's sake!

Punch said: 'So that's him, Joker. I see.'

'I will give you the count of three.' Caldeiro's mercurial temper rose abruptly. 'Then I shall shoot you down like the dogs you are.'

'That's more like the Caldeiro we know,' commented Dexter.

'No go, blokes,' said Barky. He made it harsh. He didn't want his lads killed. This Argie bastard might give them a hard time; once they'd surrendered he couldn't very well have them shot out of hand, could he?

He let his Uzi droop so that the muzzle pointed at the soggy ground. Now he thought about it, the night was decidedly unpleasant with snow on the way and a chill factor that didn't bear thinking about. But then, anything was better than thinking about the debacle going on right here and now. All the same, Barky, prone to depression that drove him on even more savagely, didn't feel at all down now. If Captain Hector Caldeiro thought he had this patrol of Strike Force to rights, snared and trapped and hopeless, then that bastard had another think coming.

'Looks like this McCartney fellow's pointing a tommy at Barky,' said Roller.

'Yeah,' said Shrimp. 'They don't look like they're very friendly.'

The two lay with their heads poking out either side of

a small bush. Their night sights revealed the scene ahead. Roller flipped out his scimitar.

'Sniper, Huey? You reading all this?'

'Yeah. Reckon that McCartney's got the drop on Barky.'

'Sniper, you might get a spot of target practice in yet.'

'Be nice,' was all Sniper had to say.

'What the hell's going on?' Rommel wanted to know.

'Looks like Barky walked into a trap,' Roller told him.

'I'm coming up.'

'Sure, Rommel, sure.'

The six men Barky had left to give cover now had to figure out the situation for themselves. Loath though they were to start shooting with their friends in the way, they knew their comrades would wholeheartedly welcome support fire if the balloon went up. Rommel could trust Barky and his patrol to hit the ground before the Argies responded.

Rommel and Woody joined the other four and they took careful stock of the proceedings ahead. They had little fear the Argies would spot them, despite the beauty and perfection of their American night sights.

'We have to let Barky make his move.' Roller sounded truculent. If Rommel started something now, and Barky and the lads copped it – no Roller wouldn't, couldn't think of that.

Well aware that he hadn't done as well as he damned well ought to have done, Rommel accepted the implied rebuke, letting it pass without comment. This time there'd be no foul-ups. 'Check,' he said in best Strike Force fashion.

Of them all Rommel was most aware of the tension of the moment, the dreadful feeling that a single wrong move could provoke a bloodbath. His mouth was dry. He must get a hold of himself. Bloody hell! He was a member of Strike Force, specially selected by the Major!

He knew, just as well as any of them, what to do.

'The second Barky gives his signal,' he said. 'Whammbo!'

Roller refrained from any comment whatsoever on this daft way of putting it. Like anyone else, Rommel had his funny little ways. Six pairs of eyes set in tiger-striped faces glared ferociously down to where their comrades faced sudden death.

Out of the side of his mouth, Punch whispered, 'I ain't standing for this –'

Dexter spoke quickly, 'Shut up, Punch.'

The breath Punch Fuller took in would have inflated a Zeppelin. He opened his mouth, snapped it shut, opened it again so that his moustache quivered, and then slammed his teeth together so they gritted.

Barky called across, 'Do I have your word that no harm will come to us in your hands, Caldeiro?'

'You have no bargaining position, Jones.'

'Oh, I wouldn't say that. You'd be gut shot for a start, that I promise.'

Caldeiro's handsome face expressed polite shock.

'I have wasted quite enough time with you. Your group has caused me considerable trouble.'

'Embarrassment?'

'Enough for me to enjoy your stupidity in falling into my trap.'

'So there never was a kelper called McCartney?'

'Of course not!'

'And the charts of the minefields around Stanley?'

Caldeiro moved his shoulders in a Latin shrug of complete indifference. 'From what I understand, there are millions of mines scattered everywhere, nobody really knows where they all are. I do not envy your soldiers when they try to march through them.'

'Now just a minute,' rapped out Barky. 'Now just hold on, Caldeiro. D'you mean to say your people have laid mines all over the place and haven't kept any records?'

'So I am given to understand. I enquired when I set up this plot. Now stop this talking and put your hands up properly, or –'

'That's uncivilised!' yelped Barky. 'That's downright dangerous and barbaric. D'you call yourselves a proper civilised lot? What an apology for soldiers!'

He stuck his left hand up in the air, and waved it up and down at right angles.

Caldeiro was no fool. He hit the ground at about the same time as Barky and his men.

The storm of gunfire that lashed across the open space struck six of the still standing Argie Special Forces personnel, knocking them over, and stalked on to the rest. The assault came from the six Britons stationed to give covering fire. Barky unhitched his Uzi and squirted a few rounds in the general direction of Caldeiro. Dexter's IW spat flame. Punch did not shoot.

Bullets slogged soggily into the turf about them. Everybody kept very low indeed.

One of the Argies was squealing like a rabbit in a snare.

'Poor sod,' said Dexter to himself, and turned to where Punch should have been at his side.

There was no sign of the big fellow.

It was useless for Dexter to fume. Punch was off on his own special brand of devilry, and nothing and nobody would stop him now. Correction. There was one thing and one person that could. That thing was the living entity known as Special Strike Force. And the person was Major Dan Granville.

Barky was yelling again, giving away his position hunkered down to the damp ground in the dimness. He yelled and then rolled away to a fresh place offering cover.

'Caldeiro! The game's up. Surrender yourself and your men now before you are all killed.'

The beautiful English voice shouted back with a trace of South American Spanish giving the accent a certain piquant charm that, according to Dexter, ought to be stuffed down the bastard's throat.

'Never! You have no chance, Englishman. *You* give *yourself* up. Now.'

'Get stuffed, you Argie creep!' bellowed Dexter and then let off a burst of fire in the direction of Caldeiro's voice.

Instantly, the Joker Dexter was squirming away to a fresh fold in the ground. The twinkle of SMG fire and the staccato of return fire sent a spray of slugs close to the position he had just vacated.

'You'll have to do better'n that, you Argie creeps,' Dexter said to himself. 'And where the hell's that benighted idiot Punch gone now?'

He started to work his way forward, moving very quietly and very carefully, folding his body into the folds in the ground flatter than a pancake.

Fire from the covering party had now ceased. All their targets were either shot down or had gone to ground.

The wounded Argie had stopped screaming and was now moaning and sobbing. Distressing as it was, this could not be allowed to upset a fellow as he set about malletting the rest of them.

One of the Argie's nerves broke. He scrambled up and started to run. Two brief bursts from SS and Dingle chopped him down.

'Chuck it in, Caldeiro,' called Barky, again.

There was no reply.

No further fire from the hostiles interrupted the proceedings. Barky pondered. He wasn't absolutely sure that they had all been hit. The fact that Caldeiro refused to answer the demand for his surrender could mean a number of things. He could be dead, he could be foxing, he could have managed to wriggle his evil self out of it. However, despite this, Barky couldn't afford to hang about much longer. All this gunfire so near Stanley was bound to bring out inquisitive hostile patrols.

So far, neither side had thrown a grenade. If that disgusting white phosphorus cloud drifted over the scene they'd all be in trouble. Barky thumbed up his scimitar.

'Disengage,' he said, quietly. 'Pull back. Want to be clear of the area by daylight.'

'Check,' came the various replies. Nothing came in from Punch Fuller.

'Punch?'

'There's no Argies around here,' came in SS's voice. 'Joker? What you done with the big feller?'

Dexter had halted his forward progress when Barky's order came over his wireless. Now he made a face to himself. What had *he* done with Punch!

'Gone off for a leak, I expect.'

'Too right.'

'Wrap it up,' snapped Barky. 'Get moving.'

The arranged first rally point a hundred metres or so from the covering party gave them time to regroup and catch their breath.

Barky looked at the other four. Deadly was holding up well, which was only natural and to be expected. SS and Dingle were their usual tough and obstreperous selves. Jack the Joker Dexter's ferocious face betrayed nothing of his concern for his oppo.

About to make a footling remark, Barky stopped. Through the gloom a bulky figure appeared, crouched over and oddly humped and lumped, like a demented camel.

'Punch?'

'Here,' said Punch Fuller, dumping his sack-like bundle onto the peaty ground. 'Here's the old bugger himself.'

Captain Hector Caldeiro flopped out, an unconscious lump of near-humanity. 'Clipped him on one side of the ear,' explained Punch.

He did not explain how his trigger finger had trembled and how the muzzle of his SMG, centred on Caldeiro as he tried to squirm away, seemed to hypnotise him. He'd almost shot the man. He'd almost let him have it. But he hadn't. He couldn't really explain it to himself, could Punch Fuller, not yet. He might understand his actions one day, actions that to him seemed irrational, but not now.

'So that's him,' said Deadly. 'Well, the Good Lord has spared him for a greater wrath to come.'

Maybe that had been in Punch's mind when he hadn't malletted this specimen who had so maltreated the Joker.

'I don't doubt the human rights people will want to have a word with him when we get him back,' said Barky. 'Ask him about all the people whose disappearance he's instigated in Argentina. Poor folk that he's tortured and murdered. They'll want to know quite a bit.'

'Yeah,' said Dingle. 'And like that other creep they'll let him go.'

'Probably.' Barky pondered. To kill Caldeiro now was quite out of the question. To take all the trouble to drag him back, for nothing in all probability, seemed hardly worth the effort. Yet just to let him go? Tamely to leave him to go back to further devilry? No, that didn't seem the right course, either.

He made up his mind.

'Take him along. And, Punch, when he wakes up, you may have a few words with him. Remind him of his position. I don't want him giving us any trouble.'

Punch opened his mouth.

Dexter said, 'Oh, he won't give any trouble. I can promise you that.'

CHAPTER FIFTEEN

Barky felt the rope in his gloved fists with some satisfaction. He was good with ropes. As he abseiled down the side of the hotel he felt compact, in control.

His target was the bedroom in which – so the best intelligence suggested – Gunjepoo was lying, trussed and gagged on the bed.

Coming down just after him and on the other side, Deadly shared his competence. Together, like eagles swooping on their prey, they booted off from the wall and then roared back and in through the window in a smashing eruption of glass and splintered wood.

On the opposite roof Noggy and Pugsy swooped down in exactly the same fashion. They crashed through their window a floor lower and landed amid a smother of glass.

Together, Smyjo and Andy broke cover from the bushes on their side of the hotel and sprinted for the French windows. They went through these swiftly, the sharp edges of the glass failing to cut through their protective clothing. Then, turning a right angle in the corridor they ran for the two entrances to the dining room and bar.

Over on the other corner of the hotel where the

terrorists took turns to sleep in a small lounge, Q and the Whizz Kid made a less spectacular entry through the already opened windows.

Out in the front with his 7.62 mm L42A1 nicely and comfortably supported on sandbags brought in for the job, Sniper took up his position and looked through the scope. Of course he always thought of his sniper's rifle as a Lee Enfield. Well, it was, really. He'd knock out the eye of a bee, his comrades said.

Now he watched as the Major, wearing a white apron and carrying a tray, approached the glassed front door of the hotel. He carried no firearms.

Everyone's movements were timed to coincide: the time the Major took to reach the glass front door; the time it took Barky and Noggy to abseil down to their respective windows; the time needed by Smyjo and Andy to cover the distance to the French windows; and the time Q and the Whizz Kid needed to scuttle up to their open windows exactly tallied. To the second.

The front porch was guarded as Superintendent Bell had indicated. One terrorist stood by the inner door with an SMG held loosely, the muzzle pointing to the tiled porch floor.

The first guard opened the glass doors with his left hand, his right holding his SMG upright in the air. It looked impressive, of a piece with the all-black fancy dress and stocking masks. In the Major's eyes they looked pathetic.

Yet he knew they were killers, desperate and merciless. Their appearance might be pathetic to a professional, but in their own dark ways they were professionals too, and must be dealt with on that basis.

In badly-accented English, the guard snarled out, 'Hurry up.'

'All right, all right,' whined the Major in a splendid imitation of fear-filled intimidation. 'I'm coming.'

He reached the two steps. He trod up the first, then the second and extended the tray past the opened glass door. He caught a nostril-full of the man's smell, pungent and foreign, mingling with the sweat of apprehension. He didn't think the fellow was actively frightened; just apprehensive and jumpy.

The terrorist, instead of reaching for the tray, jerked his left hand down.

'On floor.'

With complete subservience the Major bent down. He moved himself slightly sideways so that the first terrorist obscured him from the view of the second. He put the tray down on the floor.

Then the Old Man rose – surging up with such stunning violence that the terrorist's neck was against one palm, the side of his head against the other before he knew what was happening. The Major twisted. The crack was dull and soggy; it was enough.

Dropping down onto one knee the Major saw the guard at the door try to swing his SMG up, startled out of his wits. Then he fell. Sniper's 7.62 mm round drilled clean through one eye.

Scooping up the sub-machine gun, the Major took the single spare magazine the fellow had stuffed into his side pocket. He roared in through the inner door into the hallway and reception area.

Up the drive hared Ickey Frost, Huey and Bunce, with Sniper slinging his rifle and belting along after them. He swung his own Uzi down into his fists and fairly hurled himself along. He wasn't going to miss this, no by God!

In the small lounge one terrorist was half asleep on a

large sofa while another cleaned his Armalite. Q and the Whizz kid sprayed bullets ahead of them. Both terrorists fell. Making sure they were out of action, the two men of Strike Force checked the hallway, then rapidly made for the dining room and bar area.

Smyjo and Andy broke through their doors at the same time and went in with Uzis aimed, their fingers pressed against the triggers.

There were four terrorists present, and two went down at once. The others made a desperate scramble for their weapons but were cut down as the sub-machine guns fell to the floor. Andy and Smyjo were left contending with the hysterical babble and yell of the hotel staff.

Q and the Whizz Kid belted in and the four members of Strike Force made a very thorough check of everyone. They could not afford to miss a terrorist in disguise.

By this time the noise of gunfire had alerted everyone. The Major, in the reception area, saw two terrorists appear at the head of the stairs and begin the descent. He shot them both in brief, deadly accurate burst of fire. Then he started up the stairs himself.

Ickey Frost's patrol burst in through the front door past the two bodies there and went leaping after the Major.

They'd been warned to expect about a dozen terrorists. That was the best intelligence the police had been able to come up with. People in this kind of trade always tried to keep their numbers secret, to prevent the authorities from learning just how many terrorists were holding hostages.

Noggy and his patrol came across only one man in the black uniform. They quickly chopped him down and raced up the stairs to join up with Barky's lot.

When Barky and Deadly crashed into the bedroom the smash of glass ripped away the curtains and allowed light to enter. The place had been in semi-gloom, the curtains drawn.

A man was sitting in an easy chair reading a magazine and smoking a cigarette. His stocking mask was pushed up over his forehead. He looked up in shocked amazement before being thrown backwards and over the back of the chair by a blast of gunfire.

Barky rushed across to the bed. Deadly yanked the door open and then stood to the side, checked and then dived out flat.

As Barky saw the bound figure lying on the bed and noticed the blood stains on the pillow, Trampas and Roller abseiled down and followed through the shattered window.

'That's him,' said Barky.

Without speaking Trampas and Roller moved towards the bedroom door.

Noggy just reached the top of the stairs before Pugsy. He knew Spider and Lawless would be following.

The hotel smelt of polish, food and static electricity. It looked nice and comfortable. The carpets were thick, and deadened his foot falls for which he was profoundly thankful. Even above the crescendo of gunfire from the bedroom along the corridor, the black-garbed figure ahead must have heard their approach.

Noggy swung his Uzi up and then checked. Deadly Dennis suddenly appeared flying flat out of the door and sprawled on the carpet. Deadly saw them. He saw the terrorist reach down to his waist for the automatic pistol belted there. Deadly yelled.

'You've had it, sunshine. If you draw that pistol

you're dead.'

Clearly the terrorist had been on his way to the bedroom to check on Gunjepoo. He would be the leader. The black-uniformed figure hesitated.

Deadly and Noggy could not fire. Their spray of bullets might cut down the hostile, but those slugs would certainly carry on to wound or kill themselves too.

For a moment no one moved.

Then, slowly and with one hand, the terrorist drew his pistol. He threw it down on the carpet. As he did so he took from his upper breast pocket a small radio and pressed the red button.

Then, like the Archangel Gabriel the Major was on the scene. 'Handcuff him, then,' said the Major. His flinty eyes and cold voice indicated his displeasure with this outcome. He did not like gunning down a man like this in cold blood. The idiot had contrived to get himself captured instead of killed. He was now an encumbrance. The only bright spot was that he would not be the responsibility of Strike Force.

The Major checked the state of Gunjepoo. He looked fat, dissolute, and unpleasant. He'd been stuffed full of drugs and would probably have no idea of what had been going on since his kidnapping.

'Free him and get him outside. Now let's have a word with this specimen of sub-human terrorism.'

The terrorist said in a high-pitched voice, 'You have about ten minutes. That is all.'

'Plenty of time,' said the Major, and his voice rang full and rich, very jovial.

The Whizz Kid went past looking extremely evil. The Major looked at him, shook his head and said: 'No, WK. Not this time.'

The terrorist reiterated, 'You don't seem to understand the position.' He swore nastily at them.

'Oh?'

'There is a bomb in the furnace room, together with the manager and his wife.'

Just as these words were spoken Smyjo appeared roaring up the stairs and along the corridor. He heard.

'So that's where they are. They weren't with the others and we were searching. I'll get down there right away,' and he was off flying down the stairs.

The Major pointed at the terrorist whom Barky had handcuffed with the set he'd borrowed from the friendly police sergeant.

'Bring him along. Move!'

Barky stepped up, got a grip on the fellow's neck and the idiot tried to kick him in the groin. Barky slid sideways, took the foot in his fist, twisted, and dumped the hostile on his nose onto the carpet.

'Wally,' he said, and bent and put his arm about the fellow to haul him up. His hand felt a soft roundness he recognised at once. They might be small; but they were there.

'A bleeding female,' he said, disgustedly.

Still, in this game that made no difference. The leader being a woman could very easily make this gang even more dangerous. One other terrorist was picked up in the lavatory, and they all trooped down to the basement. Deadly pulled the black balaclava off and a close-cropped head of black hair was revealed. Her face was hard, experienced, and could have been quite pretty without the bitter twist to the lips. All the same, Barky reminded himself, evil though these people were, they must believe, if not in what they were doing, then at least in themselves.

The manager and his wife, ordinary citizens caught up in a situation of pure horror, were in a pitiable state. They were untied and their gags removed and, before they could create too much of a scene, Sawbones turned up to take care of any wounded.

'You have about five minutes,' said the lady terrorist.

'Plenty of time, plenty of time,' boomed the Major in a deliberately cheerful way. 'So that's the bomb. Interesting. We'll just –'

The Whizz Kid spoke. 'You shift that, Major, and bang.'

'Ah!'

The girl terrorist laughed.

The manager, distraught, said, 'My hotel! It will be destroyed –'

'Outside with 'em, Sawbones.'

No one bothered to mention that one hotel and one life were mere nothings in the scale of these people's importance.

The bomb sat on the floor beside the furnace, squat and unpleasant. The Major beamed at the girl.

'I expect you understand all about this little beauty, don't you? Of course you do. Handcuff her by the flaming bomb, Barky. Now, my dear, if you don't defuse it then – well, I'm expecting you to sacrifice your life for your principles. Bye bye hotel. Now, blokes, all out.'

'You can't do this! You devil, you're more inhuman than –'

'Quite so, quite so. All out. Move!'

Outside Smyjo said, 'The Whizz Kid was itching to have a go at that bomb, Major.'

'Of course. And it was itching to have a go at him. No, old son. She knew how to defuse the doohickey. The Whizz Kid would have taken more than four minutes.

Which reminds me – she must have done it, or it would have gone up by now.'

Then Barky yelped out, 'Look there! There's Guy, and Punch and the Joker. And that's Vadim they've got with 'em.'

The new arrivals walked across from their car.

'That's right,' said Guy. 'Dashed interesting, you know. This blighter Vadim came here, so we nabbed him. Neat, what?'

'Pity,' said Roller, glaring, 'he wasn't already inside.'

'Now, now, Romeo,' said Trampas. 'You're frightening the poor sod.'

The Major spelled it out for them. 'See this miserable specimen, Vadim. He is staring at you. He sees men he tangled with. Don't you think he has every right to be scared right down to his socks?'

And, looking at Strike Force in that moment, you couldn't say fairer than that.

Barky wondered, down in the South Atlantic, if Captain Hector Caldeiro experienced the same kind of fear when he looked at the men of Strike Force. He had tricked them and tried to trap them. They had taken him prisoner. Well, he knew only too well what he did to prisoners – if he expected a little of his own medicine they might not be in too much of a hurry to dispell that misguided notion.

The mine problem, they soon discovered, was real. Horrifyingly real. Both Argentinian army and marines had laid mines uncaring of what the other did. Mines had been laid by various units simply to protect themselves; they could be anywhere. Some records had been made, but they conflicted. Many markers had disappeared. No one in Strike Force envied the marine and para Royal Engineers in this humane and yet dismaying task.

As Barky phrased it for them all: *Bloody mines!'* Apart from the tragedy of having sheep and cattle blown up by the mines, and vehicles too, the most wretched aspect was that the people of the Falklands, the kelpers, would not be able to resume a normal way of life.

As for the thought that kiddies could go happily off to play where they'd always gone off to play ... – No. Oh, no, that gave everybody nightmares.

There were bombs among the mines, and diabolical booby traps. Stanley itself contained so much ammunition the stuff was piled up and lay beside smashed cases all round the town.

But, it was the mines that caused the nightmares. *Bloody mines.*

By the time they all congregated in Port Stanley, Strike Force, or what was left of it, felt the weight of their exertions burdening them in a way that the enormous physical loads they had carried hacking over the Falklands never had done. Each Wing now found out what the others had been up to. Some of the personnel of Number Four Wing were still to come in. They learned that Captain Tom Burnaby had been wounded by a sniper.

They wanted to go to SS *Uganda* to see the Major and find out how he was progressing. When they'd cleared up the Gunjepoo operation and were on their way back to HQ, someone had passed a scathing comment about him. Gunjepoo had not even thanked them for saving his skin. Instead, he'd raved and accused them of treachery, threatening to have a contract put on them.

He'd calm down by reason and conviction of the Foreign Office, in the end, no doubt. The Major surprised them, 'Old Gunjepoo? Oh, he's a very well-balanced personality.'

'Well-balanced!'

'Sure. He's got a chip on each shoulder.'

'They'd done him in the eye in the end though, as, being hellions from Strike Force, they'd been certain to do. But, of course, no one was going to talk about *that*.

Now, as they rested up in the abandoned house Q had requisitioned for their use, they could start to get the shakes about all the stupid, reckless things they'd done during the campaign. Operation Corporate and other operations had created their own legends. The 'True Glory' rested with the men of the Task Force, the pilots, the Marines and Paras, the Guards and Gurkhas and all the support arms. And the Merchant Navy sailors who'd carried the lads here through hostile seas. All the men and women who'd had a hand in fashioning this victory out of impossible odds – to them the palms, to them the laurels, to them the 'True Glory'.

Talking the course of events over, Strike Force came to the conclusion that it didn't really matter who sank whose ship first. If an enemy vessel was sniffing around your supply ships and transports, not to speak of your escorts and carriers, then you'd sink the blighter if you could no matter which way she was heading. The idea of Exocets and large-calibre shells thunking into *Invincible* or *Hermes* or any of their ships at all brought out the shudders.

No doubt the various cover stories floated by the two antagonistic governments at the time appeared to them to be logical and sensible. Perhaps one day the truth might come out. Or the Argies might chuck their government out and get in a new lot. The men of Strike Force could only hope that they would be amenable to reason. But one thing they knew.

If they had to come down here and chuck the Argies

out of their stolen islands for a second time, they'd do it. But this time it would be far more difficult ...

As Punch Fuller put it: 'We'd have to give 'em the big Fish and Chip elbow again.'

'Check,' said Jack the Joker Dexter.

And Roller, 'Suck 'em in like Vadim.'

'The old Gunjepoo op,' confirmed Barky.

Captain Tom Burnaby walked in on the exchange, his arm in a sling, yet brisk, urgent and incredibly tough.

'Yeah,' he said. 'Strike Force has come of age. We might be an evil-minded bunch, but we go up against the bad guys all the time.'

That was what he said. What he thought was that Claire and Anne might take a little delicate handling by the time he got back to England. He'd used Strike Force techniques to clear up a business there that was not too dissimilar. If people went around pinching other people's property and trying to ride roughshod over them, somewhere there had to be a redress, an answer. There ought to be some factor like Strike Force, surely?

'Right,' said Captain Tom Burnaby. 'We've got our sailing orders. Saddle up.'

They were leaving good men down here in the Falklands. Jock and Stumer, and Pugsy. They'd be leaving Bunce's foot. Some of them were wounded. Well, hell, and what did you expect when you got into a shooting war? Sweet violets?

In the future there would be plenty of opportunities for Special Strike Force to don their white hats and go riding off to the rescue of poor unfortunates. That was their destiny. That was why they'd been created.

'We'll go across and see the Major,' Burnaby told them all. 'And then we're going home.'